Death Is Not Always Silent
from
The SICARDO's Files

A Novel
by
Oliver Sims

Death Is Not Always Silent from the SICARDO's Files,
soft-cover edition 2019

ISBN: 9781080299874

For more information about special discounts for bulk purchases, please
contact us: bpcpublishing@gmail.com

Cover Design: Alberto Ponte
Cover Photo: Ibarionex Perrello

Bellucci, Palms & Carmichael Publishing, LLC

Dedication

To my loving wife Juanita Palacios-Sims, for having my back and saw me as a writer from the very start.

Iris Sims my beloved mother who gave me the gift of life and taught me "Treasure of The Heart."

Daisaku Ikeda, President of the Soka Gakkai International (Value Creation Society), my mentor. Through his inspirational writings and personal examples, taught me, by faith, practice and study, one can make the impossible, possible.

Acknowledgments

This book would not have been possible without the assistance and guiding light of my editor, agent and true friend Michael Perrotta. His unwavering belief in me and patience was remarkable.

The stories from the Sicardo Files are fictional crime novels however; detective Federico Sicard, a retired Detective Supervisor for the Los Angeles Police Foreign Prosecution Interpol Liaison Unit, was the canvas and backdrop for developing and creating the story. As my consultant he provided authenticity to the novel.

Los Angeles Detective Regina Crenshaw is a no nonsense female pistol packing law enforcer. I greatly appreciated our dialog and her input as a female detective in a dominated male aggressive world, both within and outside the law.

1

Moments of ease and light heartedness were rare for Leon, every time he would spend those special minutes with Sophia, though, he would forget the drama and trauma that he was faced with every day at home.

But the hardest thing he faced was his "goodbye" to her. That late evening Leon's family was scheduled to move from Cali to Cartagena. His stepfather had received a promotion and Leon had no choice but to adhere to his wishes.

At fourteen, Sophia was "his girl." A few months prior, Leon had turned fifteen, but with all the other things he had to contend with, at times he felt as if he were fifty years old.

He was glad, for on that last day, he had been able to spend most of the time with her. The sorrow of leaving and not knowing when he'd see her next, was eating him inside. He tried to be upbeat and kept reassuring her that as soon as possible he'd visit her.

The day was hot and humid; they were walking back to Sophia's house after swimming in the nearby river in the jungle. They took the shortcut through the clearing where the Linstrem's cattle grazed about on the green pasture.

Leon and Sophia talking, laughing and flirting with one another made their way toward her house.

"My *papi* said you are a good young man."

"He hardly knows me!"

"He knows you take care of your mom, your sister and you had even taken care of your... *papa*." She pronounced "papa" with hesitation.

"What about my *papi*?" Leon asked in a defending tone.

"Well... your mom, your... papa, when... he used to get drunk."

Leon stopped and took Sophia's hand, "I'll protect you also."

"Will you?"

"I will always."

"Say it."

"My Sophy, you know I'll protect you forever and a day."

"No, say it as if you mean it."

"I, Leon Sicardo, will protect Sophia Linstrem with my life."

She smiled and gave him a kiss on his cheek, "You are my prince until the end of time."

Approaching the barn by Sophia's house, they saw her father surrounded by three soldiers.

She detected something was not right by the way her father shook his head in disapproval at the three men.

One of the soldiers walked over to a cow and began examining the animal, stroking it and then said something to Ludwig, Sophia's father.

Because of the distance Leon and Sophia couldn't hear what was being said.

"I hate them," said Sophia, as she let go of Leon's hand and began quickening her pace towards her father.

One of the soldiers reached for his gun and pointed it at Ludwig's head.

Sophia's rapid stride became a full-out sprint, even though, the knee-high wheat field made running difficult.

When she was at approximately hundred yards from the men, the same soldier, with the butt of his gun struck Ludwig's face sending him to the ground.

"*Papi!*" Sophia shrieked.

Her voice became imprinted on Leon's ears.

The soldiers turned in her direction and one of them fired his gun.

Leon fell, hitting the ground hard.

"Don't shoot, get them," commanded the Sargent.

Sophia turned and saw Leon get up. He had tripped over an overgrown long root of a mango tree.

"Run Leon!" she yelled in his direction.

The two men rushed toward him.

Instinctively, Leon ran in the opposite direction towards the woods. He attempted to bolt forward but the high grass slowed him down. He saw the trees ahead, which would shroud, eventually swallowing him into the secretive jungle.

"I got to get to the river." He kept telling himself, never once looking back.

The dense bushes by the river's bank, the thick vegetation and the shrubs with their sharp pointed thorns slashed his face, others lancing his arms, still others lacerating his legs like cuts of razor-blades.

He could hear the soldiers rapidly approaching behind him. He felt that tingling fear on the back of his neck, motivating him to run even faster.

He kept thinking, 'Get to the river. Get to the river.'

Scared, breathing hard, running faster, it was finally in sight, Leon could now hear the grumble of rushing water.

In full stride he leaped off the bluff.

He then heard the sound of a second bullet echoing in mid-air.

~

The tranquil middleclass neighborhood of Culver City, nestled between Baldwin Hills, Marina Del Rey and the college community of USC, was disrupted by people scurrying about trying to avoid the looming downpour. Drivers in their cars plotted along in bumper to bumper traffic; at 5:12PM the menacing clouds had turned the gray day into what was becoming the dark of night.

The roar of thunder was heard in the far distance.

Terry Mitchell finally arrived home from work after having driven through that nerve-grinding commute. He could hear the snail-like pace of each tiny drop of water hitting the roof of his SUV.

The increasing rhythmic pattern from the sound of the rain reminded him when he would beat his hands against his desk, making believe he was playing his bongo.

He slowly drove the SUV all the way up the driveway. He parked it under the port in its usual spot then turned off the engine.

Terry not concerned at all about the storm, sat back making himself more comfortably in his black-on-black Lincoln Navigator; blasting from the CD player, the Bon Jovi's song, *Livin' on a prayer.*

He strummed on an imaginary guitar and with exaggerated up-and-down head-bobbing motions kept pace to its rock music... feeling no pain.

'I can't believe that I can't crank up the music like this in my own home,' he thought.

On the other hand, his wife Lucinda of fourteen years and Camille his adoring daughter, enjoyed mostly ranchero and mariachi music, from his wife's home town of Playa Del Carmen, Mexico.

His daughter's taste at times was opposite of her mother's. Being a teenager and influenced by her peers, hip-hop was her favorite.

Terry's solo rock performance was interrupted by the ringing of his cell. He reached for his coat on the passenger seat and answered it, while he pushed the CD player button, "off."

Terry's demeanor and body language changed immediately upon hearing a coarse but smooth unemotional voice.

"I told you I'll make it happen but you have to be patient. I need a little more time," rattled Terry.

"Terry, that's what you've been telling me but my boss has run out of what you call 'patience.'"

Frightened, "I'll get it, don't worry. I give you my word."

"Terry... Terry... we don't want your words. You know exactly what we want. And we want it now!" He emphasized "NOW!"

The cell went silent, so did Terry's mind.

A loud thunderous boom like the sound of a shot-gun blast undulated an electrical-discharge through his pounding heart. Terry screamed out loud.

He looked at his chest and with his hands, patted himself, trying to find a wound that might have been left by what he thought to be a bullet. A few moments later he realized there were no entry wounds or blood spewing from his body.

The only down-pour; was rain. It was coming down hard.

He said out loud, "How in hell did I wind up here?"

Lucinda, as she looked through the kitchen window saw her husband sitting in the SUV, motionless with a look of fear on his face.

She knocked hard on the glass and signaled for him to come inside. With her hands she mimicked with jests to cover and protect his head from the deluge.

He looked up and gave her a gentle wave back.

Lucinda couldn't know that the smile he flashed was a sham.

～

An unusually warm weather for April on Malibu beach, even though 78 degrees and clear sunny skies, did not affect the frigid Pacific Ocean. Only a few kids waded in and out of the water as several diehard surfers rode the waves.

Saturday, Herman Stein and Tiffany Stern in their mid-twenties walked along the northern end of the beach. For the third time that week, they picked-up on the dreaded conversation.

"Tiffy, we've been over this a thousand times; I don't want us to live in a one bedroom apartment."

"Yeah-Yeah."

"Tiffy, how many times do I have to tell you... I'm waiting to receive my promotion with a hike in pay."

"As a local cable operator how much more are they going to give you?"

"First of all, I'm not a cable operator but an assistant in the sales department. Second, my promotion will make me an Account Executive, more money."

"Herman, at times I get the feeling you don't want to marry me."

"I do, I do Tiffy."

"It's just that I love you so much Herman Stein and I will take you as you are."

"Las Vegas here we come, baby."

She giggled, then hugged and gave him a kiss on his cheek. She suddenly stopped and removed her sunglasses.

"What is it, Baby?"

"Look, there." She pointed to a small light-brown wooden box, fifteen yards in front of them.

As Herman wiggled the box out of the wet sand, Tiffany asked, "What is it?"

"I don't' know but it's got some weight to it."

"Break it open," impatiently instructed Tiffany.

Herman on his knees brought the box to his chest and with his right hand tried forcing it open.

Turning to her, he said, "Look for a rock or stick... something." He struggled trying opening it.

She handed him a smooth rock the size of a fist.

He immediately hammered on the box.

"It's not working."

Frustrated he went to look for a bigger stone.

While he was gone, Tiffany went at it trying to unhinge it.

She heard him say, "This should do it."

Herman had come back holding a midsized boulder.

He slammed it down on the box cracking it open. From it he pulled out a copper urn.

"We got a genie in the bottle. Let's make three wishes..." He broke out in a laugh.

"I'm getting a negative vibe from this," said Tiffany, nervously.

In a spooky vampire voice, he said, "Ooh it's someone's ashes."

"Herman please, don't make fun...."

On the lid cover he read the engraved letters; PROPERTY OF LOS ANGELES CORENER OFFICE.

They looked at each other.

"Throw it back into the ocean, please!"

"Don't be afraid, silly."

"Don't *ever* make fun *at* death."

2

Two months earlier, James and Leon, two detectives from the LAPD, lowered their heads as they passed underneath a yellow police barricade tape. Walking across the front yard, soggy from the night's rain, they made their way up the front porch.

James, who had a barely noticeable limp in his walk, asked Leon, "Why do you think the lieutenant had us, come down here, as if we don't have enough shit on our plate?"

"Your guess is as good as mine, all I know, it's unusual to have something like this come down in this neck of the woods."

They approached the front entrance and showed their badges to the posted officer.

"I'm Los Angeles Police Detective Leon Sicardo."

"And I am Detective James McCooly."

"How can I help you, detectives?"

"Can you point us in the direction of Detective Rodger Englehart?" asked James McCooly.

"Can you give us heads-up on what happened here?" asked Leon.

"We have three vics inside."

"Were you the first officer on the scene?" inquired Leon.

"No, Officer Stephen Blunt was the first to discover the bodies."

"Thanks," McCooly said.

"You'll find Detective Rodger Englehart upstairs in one of the bedrooms." The officer pointed in the direction.

"Could you guys sign in? My Sargent is a real stickler when it comes to the crime scene log-in sheet."

Under other already scribbled names and badge numbers on the log, they wrote theirs.

Before stepping inside the two-story house, they looked closely at the door and seeing that there were no signs of forced entry, they proceeded through a narrow hallway.

McCooly chewed his gum as he looked at marking #1. He started immediately to take notes: *Mud stains leading from the living room into the hallway and onto the stairs.*

Leon observed the portraits and several photographs of family outings. They were neatly hanging from a wall that lead upstairs.

McCooly noted marking #2: *a broken white and yellow candle. Spilled wax on floor. A broken picture frame. Nearby, shattered crystal vase. Dispersed sunflowers fallen from a waist-high end-table. All the above scattered at bottom of stairs.*

Leon commented, "Only in LA can you find sunflowers in the middle of February." Then he thought, 'What else is out of place? Whatever he or she leaves, even unconsciously, will serve as a silent witness against them.'

McCooly broke Leon's thoughts, "How did the perp or perps get in?"

Officer Stephen Blunt, who was wearing his elastic gloves not to contaminate evidence, chimed in from the kitchen, "The back door glass panel was broken. Nothing seems oddly out of place…"

He was interrupted by footsteps being heard coming down the stairs, it was Medical Examiner Ms. Shuchun Liang, who immediately greeted them.

Highly intelligent, Ms. Shuchun had moved to Berkeley, California, where she earned her medical degree. In the last two years she had been a new addition and a great asset to the LAPD.

McCooly, always smiled with delight at seeing her. He'd also flirt with her and whenever he had a chance would made sure to call her "Diane." He'd been in love once with a woman by the same name. However, neither Diane's reciprocated his feelings.

"Hey Diane, how you doing?" greeted McCooly. "We've got to find a better way to meet." He gave her a seductive smile.

"We received a special invitation from our neighbors in blue, here in Culver City." Leon said, very professionally.

"What are we dealing with?" Asked McCooly.

"You'll see once you get upstairs. Detective Englehart will brief you. Excuse me but I need to retrieve something from my van."

Detective Englehart, who was standing at the top of stairs, asked, "Are you detectives McCooly and Sicardo?"

"At your service." responded Leon.

"Are you Englehart?" questioned McCooly.

"Yeah, come on up."

With every step they took, Leon could smell the scant rancid malodor as he approached the middle of the stairs. Unfortunately he had smelled this many other times before and as he reached the top of the stairs it became very pronounced.

"I really don't fucking know why you're here on my case." Said Englehart indignantly.

"Yeah, well, fuck this, as if we don't have enough shit of our own," said McCooly heatedly.

"I really get pissed when brass shoves things down my throat."

"We're just following orders, you're in charge man," calmly said Leon.

"Gentlemen, let me take you to the second bedroom," said Englehart.

The putrid smell of death was present even before they stepped in.

Entering the predator's den, human waste, cut flesh and blood permeated the air making it almost difficult to breathe. What seemed an innocent precious teen's room, muddy footprints, dried brown and red splattered blood stains on the beige shag-rug revealed a horrid scene. It took a moment for Leon and James to get control of their nerves.

Seeing the lifeless bodies of a male, female and young teen, Leon stopped in his tracks. He thought,

'Must be the bodies of the mother, father and their teen-age daughter.'

The most difficult thing for him to overcome was seeing the body of the young victim, who was lying on her back with arms and legs eagle-spread tied to the bedposts.

Leon walked up to the young adolescent, placed a gloved finger on her throat and felt for a pulse. He knew there would be no blood flowing through her veins.

He thought, 'She looks so innocent... poor child.'

Her glazed-over eyes... wide opened, colorless, lifeless and her overall molested body showed the pain inflicted upon her by the killers.

Leon closed his eyes. He felt her tormented spirit speak through him. He heard her say, "No! Please don't. Help me daddy, please help me, get them off me, daddy make them stop." Leon literally heard her scream at the top of her lungs, feeling the pain she was going through.

The room was silent.

At that moment Sophia Linstrem came to Leon's mind. Saddened by this thought; he couldn't bring himself to stop thinking of her. *'Sophia was different from the other girls in her class. She had a seeking mind toward learning with the desire to become a teacher. Having blonde hair and blue eyes made her stand out among her Cali roots and having very pale complexion, she was prone to sunburns. They called her 'Pretty Red.'*

I was the only boy in the area to receive approval from Ludwig to associate with Sophia without parental supervision. I think it was because I was respectful and had manners unlike some of the other roughnecks in town.'

Leon opened his eyes and took note of the mauve colored walls with large posters of Christina Aguilera, Beyoncé and Selena Gomez. He realized this was the victim's room decorated with a young teenager's taste.

'This was her sanctuary... a place of comfort; a safe haven from the chaos in the saha world. Away from the difficulty and struggle.' He reflected for a few seconds. 'Wait a minute... In the pictures down stairs there are four people in the photos... two adults and two girls.'

"Where's the little girl?" Leon asked Detective Englehart.

"Good question," Englehart replied. "We don't know, we're searching everywhere and asking neighbors."

"From the disorder in this room there must have been an intense struggle." Interjected McCooly.

"I examined closely the muddy shoe impressions on the carpet and there were at least three other people in here besides the victims."

'Why would someone do this heinous abuse to a child?' Leon asked himself.

He went to examine the other two victims. They were bound hand-and-foot and tied back-to-back on chairs; the same as the ones in the dining room.

"The gun powder residue on the father's forehead is from a single close range bullet shot. The woman was executed in the same manner," said Englehart.

"Gangster style," commented Leon.

Medical Examiner Shuchun "Diane" Liang had returned with a small hand-held device. She turned it on then raised the bottom of the bedsheet, which covered the teenager, just by looking at the victims bruised legs, she said, "Most likely she's been raped."

The father had been positioned to face the bed and forced to watch his daughter being mutilated and brutalized. The mother had been blindfolded to face the opposite direction and could only hear the lamenting of her daughter, the creaking of the bed, the rustling of the bedsheets and the bestial grunting sounds of the rapist... and then of the second... and of the third.

'Why are these thoughts of Sophia so vivid today?' Leon asked himself.

Dr. Liang saw immediately with the ultraviolet light, the semen stains not visible to the naked eyes.

She continued, "Looks like forced vaginal penetration. But I'll have to do the usual tests in the lab to confirm."

McCooly looking at "Diane" with wanting eyes, said, "Hey Doc, I noticed the blood around the other two victims seemed thick, dry... getting hard. What can you tell us about the time line?"

"The vics have been dead for quite a while. It looks like the rigor mortis had peaked and began to slacken. I'm guessing death took place between eighteen and thirty hours ago."

Detective Englehart lowering the upper part of the bedsheet exposed the victim's chest and then stated, "You guys recognize this?"

Stunned, Sicardo and McCooly had already seen this marking on another unsolved gang and drug related murder two years prior.

The talons of a claw from a bird of prey had been inflicted on the inner side of the teenager's left breast, lacerating a three inch flesh wound.

"Drugs claim other victims than just its users," said Dr. Liang.

Leon's heart leapt vociferously like a reverberating bass drum.

Death is not always silent.

3

Eddie Cole's Tavern located on 26th and Pico Boulevard, with its film noire ambiance, vintage oak wood structures and the Pacific Dining room, had become Leon's preferred place to hang out and unwind.

After World War II, the one-of-a-kind uniquely designed bar at Eddie Cole's was purchased by an American officer stationed in Duxford, England. He had the handmade wooden structured artifact transported to his hometown of Boston, Massachusetts.

Sometime during the '70's, it found its permanent location in the city of Santa Monica. The legend of the bar has it that the six feet high shelves, which would hold the assortment of alcohol beverages was assembled from beams of a shipwrecked vessel off the shores of England in the early 1900's.

The current owner, Julio had purchased the place after Eddie's passing and kept the name Eddie Cole's in honor of his friend and mentor.

Leon sat on one of ten barstools, which surrounded the oval shaped counter, he was sipping his favorite libation, *Four Roses Single Barrel* on the rocks. To him there was nothing more satisfying than that sweet taste of good bourbon and nothing better to compliment it than a sizzling thick juicy medium-rare steak.

Leon's philosophy had always been, 'One never knows when one's time comes to an end, so enjoy life and the little things it has to offer.'

Leon Vincente Sicardo, as far back as he could remember, his father made him be proud to honor his name. "Little Lion" is how his family and friends called him ever since he was a child but as he got older they called him by his given name "León."

Being the toughest kid in the barrio, he would say, "I'm the king of the beasts, don't fuck with me and I won't have to hurt you."

At twenty, he escaped the dense hellish conditions of Cartagena, Colombia and made his way to Los Angeles, California.

The incarcerated criminals, whom he had put away over the years, out of respect would call him "The Dirty BOS."

He was proud of this label, this uncanny ability to adapt became part of his survival skill.

America wasn't easy for him but as usual he found his reprieve in swimming. He was thankful for the Junior college system making it possible for him to learn how to speak and write the new language.

He'd say to everyone, "English is not my mother's tongue."

Most people would get a kick out of this comment but for Leon everything seemed possible in the new "Promised Land." He even earned his degree and eventually became an American citizen.

Proud to be able to accomplish all he always wanted, he felt and thought, 'America is a great country.'

A recruiter referred him to the Los Angeles Police Academy. Becoming an officer of the law was foreign and improbable for him because in Colombia the Nacional Policía, to him, were all corrupt.

Leon joined the LAPD and those early years were gruesome and arduous. He'd have to constantly maneuver to over-perform and out-think blatant racist actions and remarks from his prejudiced peers and supervisors.

He left those hellish days behind possessing that special attitude of the "the lion king" never to be defeated.

His stripes were earned by being a dedicated and professional lawman. Never once did he regret joining the force.

As Leon sipped his second glass of bourbon his thought went to Sophia and the period when evil spread throughout Colombia like locusts, then his thoughts shifted to her father: *'A fourth generation German of Jewish faith left his homeland as a young boy to escape the evil regime of the Third Reich. He and his uncles escaped to Honduras to prepare the way for the remaining family members to join them, who unfortunately never made it out of Germany. All was lost. Sophia's family line began and ended with her father and her Honduran born mother. Sophia's father, Ludwig, never took*

a liking to Honduras. He had the ability to speak and adapt to languages; German, Swedish, French and some English. Adding Spanish to the repertoire was not difficult. He saved his money, set out to find new land to toil and to herd cattle. However when he moved the family to Colombia, he fell in love with the people and its geography; making it his home. Ludwig was proud and extremely protective of Sophia, his one and only child.
Her father like my father, Eduardo, had ill feelings toward FARC. Because their acts of debauchery reminded Sophia's father of the evil regime he left behind in his native homeland. Ludwig kept his thoughts to himself but those in command within the militia knew his true feelings.'

The Revolutionary Armed Forces of Colombia, known as FARC, was destroying the lives of innocent people who opposed their ideology and way of life.

The Colombian government and FARC fought each other for many years creating havoc and cataclysm on the Colombians.

The people in Cali and Melan saw FARC as an armed ruthless force whose tactics resembled that of criminals and organized gangsters. Kidnapping, extortion, drug trafficking and murder were actions for gaining money to support their political cause and to overthrow the status-quo of the Colombian government. Anyone, who spoke against FARC, received cruel, unusual punishment and even death for being outspoken. In order to bolster and demonstrate their military strength, they recruited adolescent kids.

Leon maintained a hatred for any type of criminal activities especially those of FARC's.

Leon was being escorted by the waitress to the booth he had requested.

"Where is the owner?" asked Leon.

"You mean Julio?"

"In the last few times I've been here, I haven't seen him. Is everything alright?|"

"Oh yes, he's been on an extended vacation, should be back next week."

"Cool!"

Miles Davis' classic tune "*Sketches of Spain*" filled the air as Leon had gone to sit at a booth and was now on his third *Four Roses*. Every so often, he kept looking toward the front entrance to see if his guest was arriving.

'Typical woman always making us wait.' He thought.

As he looked up once again, he saw a gentleman hold open the door for Vanessa Compose.

The man gave her a broad smile.

She smiled in a thankful way.

Leon immediately recognized her, she was after all, a local primetime television newscaster. Her skin the color of a perfect *café con leche*.

Men in upscale taverns and trendy Hollywood celebrity spots discussed her beauty, saying, "She could make a Taliban give up his gun, take faith and be *Born Again*."

Vanessa's stride was titillating and seductive. Standing at 5'8", in Christian Louboutin black décolleté shoes, she walked in. She seemed to have hovered down the aisle.

He sighed and a second later took an even deeper breath.

Leon raised his hand and waved her over to his booth. As he got up to greet her, he thought, 'Exquisite! Dangerous even for a lion king.

"I almost didn't recognize you," greeted Leon.

"Excuse my tardiness just cut my hair short."

They shook hands.

"You mean I might lose my audience?"

"Not with those gorgeous grey-green eyes."

"You're too kind Detective Sicardo."

"Please, call me Leon."

"Ok, Detect... sorry! Leon."

"What are you having?"

"A follow-up from our phone conversation..."

"Oh the urn?"

"Yes, the wooden box."

"Let's grab a bite." Leon at not hearing an answer as to whether she was staying for dinner, in a low voice, continued, "Can I call you Vanessa?"

"You can. I'm looking for some information."

Leon leaned over the table and whispered, "Between you and me, it's off the record."

Vanessa, in deep thought stared into the glass of water in front of her. She looked up straight into his eyes, "Leon... please?"

In his own thoughts, 'She's thick, more to caress. Damn! Those full voluptuous lips, it must be the cherry red lipstick... they look so inviting.'

He heard a voice seemingly coming from somewhere, "Mars to earth... Vanessa to detective Leon... are you there?"

"Lost in space for a sec."

"You were telling me..."

"Ok... It's an unsolved murder investigation."

"Murder?"

"Did you know this place has been around for over ninety years? If these walls could talk… I'm sure…"

"Yes, exactly... Give me something I can wrap my arms around."

"I can only tell you, the urn was found a couple of weeks ago. The remains of Baby Girl Righteousness."

"Who? What else can you tell me?

"Strange name, strange case."

"Leon, come on."

"The cremation took place shortly after the murder."

"And…"

"And there is nothing else." Then Leon quietly thought, 'Damn I've already said too much.'

"Leon, beside what's been given to us by the news agencies, I have to report something newsworthy."

"That's all I got sweetheart," he said in a Bogart voice.

"And the murders in Culver City?"

"What about them?"

"Rumor in the newsroom has it, it's a home invasion gone bad."

"You believe in rumors, Miss Compose?"

"Rumor also has it that you're a difficult detective, Mr. Sicardo."

"Can I buy you another drink?" Leon asked in a soft voice.

4

In Lieutenant Peter Rory's office, James McCooly and Leon Sicardo were comparing notes and debriefing the Lieutenant.

Peter Rory demanded to be called "Lieutenant" by those of lower rank-and-file within the Department or "LT." by his immediate subordinates. But by his white officers of the same rank or higher, he allowed them to call him "Pete."

Fifteen years prior, Michael Rory, Pete's father, had run the department for over 25 years and he made sure he promoted only white men who showed integrity and character. But above all, he demanded extreme loyalty from all. For him, African-Americans, Hispanics and Asians were considered second-class citizens. Women on the force were not part of his equation; accepting them only if, in secretarial roles. Once Affirmative Action became obligatory in the LAPD, for Michael

Rory this was something he could not accept... he retired.

Leon had always suspected and thought Michael Rory was forced out.

Pete ran the unit in the same manner as his father but somewhat was changing with the times. However, he had received his promotions through entitlement – after all, his father and an older brother were on the force.

A "prime" example of the good ol' boys network, in full affect.

Leon and James would always bump heads with him.

Leon... considered him "a prick." He had no flavor or as they would say in Spanish *"no savor."*

The Lieutenant only saw them as men of color having different cultures from his, but would always be overwhelmed by their tactical skills as detectives. They never failed in making "LT." look good."

McCooly and Sicardo had an innate ability to complete their assignments. They were the best at what they did; having solved many complex cases that LT. had given them... except this one.

~

McCooly was born in the less-fortunate end of Compton, California but he rose up from the hard knock pavements of that city. He straddled the line between good and bad. He learned early on, with great precision how to maneuver through the segregated and racially divided streets of Los Angeles.

James hustled and made a quick buck by any means necessary. He made reasonable amount of money selling drugs to anyone who was willing to buy; weed, pills and the likes; Cross Tops and Black Beauties.

McCooly's father was constantly in his ear about the dignity of life to be lived on the "straight and narrow." He warned his son that the path he was traveling on, would lead to incarceration or worst... death.

James McCooly, in 1968 at the age of nineteen was already fully aware of the racial covenants that prevented Black and Mexican-Americans from renting or buying houses in certain areas. Even in Los Angeles, African-Americans were being excluded from high paying jobs, affordable housing and politics.

McCooly's father, Archie, a Tuskegee Airman in World War II, even though equipped with an engineering degree could only find a job as a warehouse supervisor. Just like his father and other neighbors, McCooly also faced discrimination from those "sworn to protect and serve."

James began to identify with a group of progressive thinkers and activists. Young Turks, who were underscoring racial dignity and self-reliance for people in the black communities. They were combining elements of socialism with black-nationalism and called on African-Americans to work together to protect their rights and improve their economic and social conditions.

These young Turks with headquarters in Oakland, California, soon formed a Los Angeles chapter as well. Their focus was to patrol the black communities of Watts and Compton, monitor police activities and protect residents from police brutality.

With pride, James endorsed the "Movement for Justice" advocated by Huey P. Newton, Bobby Seale, Angela Davis and Eldridge Cleaver, most of them co-founders of the Black Panther Party for Self-Defense.

McCooly aligned with the parallel ideologies of the Panthers, who saw the unjust interventions link between America's armed participations abroad in Africa, Latin America and Vietnam.

A nerve was touched when Eldridge Cleaver heralded, "The bondage of the Negro at home, 'black people,' live in a Colony in the mother country, shunted into inferior housing, jobs and schools."

Without hesitating a moment, McCooly retracted from his mischievous, treacherous deeds, to be active in creating prosperity in his own community. Now he had a sense of belonging with pride to partake in the Black Panther's Party Children Breakfast Programs and other community services neglected by city officials.

~

El Niño played havoc with the LA weather, heavy torrential rain created a foul mood in many Angelinos.

Lieutenant Rory was in no better temperament.

In his usual manner of raving and ranting, he raised hell once again. "I'm getting my ass kicked from these goddamn politicians. The Commissioner is putting fire under it. I'm gonna put it under yours. I need some answers from you boys; on 'Baby Girl Righteousness.' I need a suspect. The media is having a field day with this."

"Why are you always addressing us as boys?" McCooly responded calmly.

McCooly and Sicardo sitting in their chairs, looked at each other trying not to laugh.

"This is exactly my point."

"What?"

"I don't give a damn about calling you guys 'boys.' Don't you understand what the hell is going on? It's about the case. We have someone with a big mouth talking about departmental affairs. When I catch that fucking bird-talking-parrot I'm going to pluck every freakin' feather off his skin."

James McCooly chuckled.

Leon remained stone faced.

McCooly adjusted his posture, crossed his legs and stated, "I still hate it when you call us boys."

Sicardo couldn't help but chuckle.

Rory flexing his muscles, shouted, "I don't give a rat's ass what you feel, McCooly."

James and Leon looked at each other in disbelief.

"I'm getting heat boys," said Rory, as he furiously clicked his ballpoint pen. He continued, "Cooly look into your neighborhood and Leon check out the Mexicans."

They looked at each other shaking their heads, bewildered.

"So Pete, you'll look into the white community then, right?" McCooly drilled Rory.

"It's Lieutenant Rory!"

"And I'm Colombian not Mexican." Said Leon pissed-off.

"Mexican, Colombian, whatever... you guys all look the same... hell you even talk the same."

"That's the problem with the system." McCooly felt rage run through his veins.

Rory looked at them. "Now that we've cleared that up, are there any new developments on Baby Girl Righteousness' case?"

"Nothing," said McCooly.

"It's as cold as the Pacific," Leon added.

"What about Culver City, Leon?"

"Are we shifting gears?"

"Yeah, summarize the Mitchell case for me."

Leon took his notepad and read: *"Terry Mitchell, age thirty four. Caucasian. He served in Iraq. Honorably discharged... Married to Lucinda, age twenty seven of Mexican descent. A family of four... three were tortured and murdered with a single gunshot to the head including their teenage daughter named Camille. And the youngest kid is missing."*

Rory interrupted, "What do you mean the 'youngest kid is missing?' How do we know that?"

"From the family portrait hanging on the wall and discussions with neighbors," said Leon.

"Damn! Any update on this?"

"No, but that's not all, the teenage daughter was raped."

"This is all fucked up. What do we have on him?"

"A prior DUI dating back seven years ago but has been clean since then. Worked at LAX at American Air as a cleaning crew supervisor. All indications show he was a responsible employee and had no known issues with the law."

"It seems to us it was a professional hit," added McCooly.

"There were markings on the young girl." Said Leon

"Apache's MO," added McCooly.

"Who's this Apache…? Is this the name you boys given him?" Asked Rory.

"Yeah," answered McCooly.

"This is the same low life, already listed as a key suspect in the drug related killings in Boyle Heights," added Leon.

"Are you guys certain?"

"Same guy with the killings, in Juarez City." Said Leon.

"Have they supplied us any information?" asked Rory.

"Yeah *you* try getting information out of Mexico," said McCooly.

"Two years ago we pegged him as a suspect on another murder," continued Leon.

Rory annoyed, "Don't we have a full name?"

"No. My feeling is, if it's Apache's work in Culver City, then we have a big problem on our hands," said Leon.

"He's a myth," McCooly continued, "You know what that means?"

"Yeah my instinct is that it might have to do with a Cartel," said Leon.

"Working with the Mexican authorities is like pulling teeth," answered McCooly.

The lieutenant nervously clicked his pen. With his left hand he wiped the perspiration from his forehead. "What else?"

McCooly read from his notes: *"Lucinda, Terry's wife - twenty seven, her maiden name was Morales. Originally from Mexico. She came to Los Angeles with her parents when she was eleven. Both parents were illegal immigrants and were sent back to Mexico. It seems she was adopted by the Sanchez family."*

"I'm still researching the information on them," said McCooly, then continued reading: *"Received a work permit and green-card seven years later. She attended and graduated from Covina-Valley High. Then off to a junior college, never completing her degree. She then met Terry Mitchell. A few years later employed by Scenic Drive Financial. She and Terry had been married for twelve years. During these years she became a US citizen."*

"Keep working your leads and let's find these fuckers," instructed Lieutenant Rory. After a minute of silence, Rory continued, "Is that it, for Culver City?"

"That's it for now." Answered McCooly.

"OK, this is what I have..." Lieutenant Rory explained, "The Baby Girl Righteousness matter will be assigned to the Cold Case Division for now. My concerns and highest priority are to develop concrete leads and establish any connections with that case to any other unsolved murders we have open. We need to find the missing child. I'll make sure to get full cooperation from Culver City.

Leon felt in his gut that there was something else beside the divulged information just discussed.

"These recent killings in Culver City have the same Glock 9. Forensics hasn't got a thing yet," explained McCooly.

"I bet you, the gun will match," said Leon.

5

James Arthur McCooly received his draft notice six months after joining the Black Panther Party. He was torn with the idea of fighting for someone's freedom in a foreign land while being enslaved to the unjust institutional racism here in his homeland of America.

McCooly loathed everything about basic training. It was agonizing for him to accept and follow orders, barked by his white commanding officers most of them from the south. They knew how to push his emotional button, causing him to retaliate. Thus receiving disciplinary punishment and extra detail duties for his defiance.

From the very first day of training-camp at Fort Ord, his outburst, laughing at fellow white recruits who were upset at having their long blond hair shaven, was hysterically funny to him. He received an excruciating painful elbow blow to his gut from the staff Sargent. On that same wet and overcast day, he got pegged for being unruly and undisciplined.

But midway through basic training, two superior officers returning from combat in Vietnam helped change the trajectory and direction of his life. And from that day on, for McCooly, it was all about becoming a soldier.

Lieutenant Calvin J. Womble, in his late twenties, son of a doctor from an upper-class black family from New Orleans spoke to McCooly with benignity to push forward.

"Your skills are exemplary. We are here to help you survive the hell that you are about to encounter. The simple act of saluting seemingly so unimportant, yet, through this simple ritual of military discipline, each man learns to respect authority and the understanding of it. In the heat of battle you may one day be called to lead other men. To command, one must learn to obey."

Sargent Major, Barton Phillips, a white country farmer with a heavy southern drawl, from Anniston, Alabama, told him, "McCooly, I survived the abyss of fire and brimstone. I'll tell you something, don't get tied into the skin game. The color of one's skin has no place in war. You must, without exception, learn how to protect your fellow brothers because underneath the skin everyone's 'blood' is red. If you want to survive, learn to protect the man next to you and he will do the same for you."

Once McCooly completed basic training, a true warrior had emerged. He took pride in wearing the uniform of his country and was well-trained to defend and protect his fellow comrades.

Having fought and having survived the infernal condition of Vietnam, he returned home a man of character and strength.

Once in the States, he found himself facing a different battle ground; questioning once again his self-identity.

Drifting from the West coast to North Carolina in search of his eradicated ancestors from Africa, McCooly found it difficult to accept this up-rooted existence created by slavery. Especially, after he had observed the people of Nam, so proud, defending for centuries their land and culture.

Having returned to what is "considered" the land of the free; he further realized the harsh, painful reminder that he was not viewed as an equal. Exasperated, his nerves on-edge knowing he was a veteran, a warrior, yet in his country he was an inferior human being.

In North Carolina, unlike the jungles of Viet Nam, the color of skin did make a difference – remaining a continuous battle for survival.

On a hot humid summer night, two white Southerners confronted him.

Foolishly, one called him a nigger.

McCooly turned and walked away.

"Boy, don't you hear me?"

McCooly kept on walking.

He felt a hand pulling him back, instinctively, he was back in Nam. He saw "the enemy" trying to bring him down. Survival was McCooly's only thought. He landed a hard punch on the man's face knocking him to the sidewalk.

The second man attempted to punch him but James was able to reach and squeeze the Southerner's esophagus leaving him grasping for air. As the first man got up, he punched McCooly in the groin. The second man coughing violently, pulled out a knife and swung slashing McCooly's army jacket.

The warning siren from a patrol car stopped the scuffle. With the police spotlight on his face, James froze.

"Don't move boy!" said one of the patrolman.

James knew better and didn't make any sudden moves or attempt to flee.

The other officer with gun drawn stood above McCooly and seeing the veteran's killer instinct, said, "Stand straight and don't move your paws."

The first officer crept up behind McCooly and with the baton struck James behind his left knee. James fell limp to the ground.

Kicked in the face, McCooly lost consciousness. Handcuffed with hands behind his back, the two officers dragged McCooly, tossing him in the back of the patrol car.

In a daze, McCooly asked for his rights.

"Where you from boy?"

"Los Angeles."

"You're a Cali boy. Hahah?" said the officer in the passenger seat.

"Nigger, you have no rights in these parts of the woods."

No other words spoken, James was taken to jail.

While in custody, he was physically and mentally abused.

After a week in jail, a local NAACP officer and a white preacher intervened on James behalf. Luckily, the preacher a Viet Nam veteran and his son, who had seen the assault, became the key witnesses in his defense. Unexpectedly, during the arraignment the judge decided to throw out the case.

McCooly immediately returned to Los Angeles.

After that incident, for many years he'd often think, 'How fortuitous, if it hadn't been for the two unlikely strangers, I would have spent years in prison most likely forgotten inside the walls of that Charlotte, North Carolina jail or worst be killed.'

This scarred him to his inner core.

James remembered the day his father counseled him, "Change poison into medicine and join the police force."

"Hell no! Never in this lifetime."

"You wore with pride the uniform to protect this country."

"And even Viet Nam was a lie." James replied in anger.

"Lie or not, protect our people. Cops are being recruited from the South to control and keep blacks in their place here in Los Angeles."

"I love you but... I can't."

"You'll make a difference, I know. Listen to me. You'll see."

∼

James took full advantage of the educational opportunities offered by the LAPD, by enrolling and earning a Bachelor of Science degree in Criminal Justice, from the University of Southern California. On several occasions he expressed a desire to earn a Master's degree in Psychology, but never pursued it.

James, even after three years of having joined the police department was still receiving a barrage of negatevity. He knew it to be racially motivated but he handled the abuse with iron-willed determination and composure.

James in turn even encouraged a fellow Latino cadet, who was struggling with the same abuse: "Not to give up." James specifically remembered telling him: "Don't be a bitch, suck it up man, you can take it. It's only bullshit and negative attitudes they are throwing at you. It's not bullets and grenades from a hostile enemy. They're only words. "

When it came to gangsters and criminals, McCooly was always extremely focused and determined. He'd take no nonsense from them. Once at gun point to his head, James told the suspect, "I'm going to give you the benefit of the doubt, do not move a muscle, as much as to blink an eye or I'll blow your brains out."

Leon was fortunate to have gotten the advice and to have such a partner, he had no doubt James would watch his back and that he'd watch James'.

~

Don Hector Guerrera called another high level cartel meeting at the bar *Del Lobo de Pradera* (The Prairie Wolf Bar.)

At the drinking well, Hector's most trusted gun totting body guards were clinging glasses and being raucous. The uproarious voices and loud Ranchero music filled the room as Temoc made his way toward the Don.

The Lieutenants out of respect moved out his way.

Hector Guerrera and Francisco Ruiz sitting at the same table sipped on their tequilas. As soon as Francisco heard that Temoc would be joining them, his face turned to fear.

Francisco had taken an extended weekend from work to be at this meeting in Mexico.

Hector expressed dismay as he took another deep drag from his cigar. Blowing smoke up into the air he looked straight into Francisco's eyes and asked, "Francisco... Francisco we have worked together for many, many years and I guess... I did not take good care of you?"

Francisco's hand shook as he pulled away from his lips the tiny glass of tequila he was sipping from. He lowered his gaze, then said, "No, Don Guerrera, you have treated me and my family very good."

The Don blew smoke into Francisco's face and violently slammed his hand on the table, making the half-filled bottle topple on its side spilling the tequila. The bottle slowly rolled off the table shattering on the floor at Temoc's feet. This startled the two servicing waitresses.

Seething with anger, the Don shouted, "*Puta*, why is it that you've become so sloppy in your work?"

Mano "Temoc" Gutierrez with his right hand in one smooth motion withdrew his Glock from his left side coat-holster. With eyes as cold as ice, Temoc pointed the gun at Francisco's head.

One could hear a pin drop.

Hector continued, "Our operation only works if everyone does their job correctly."

Francisco sweating and with a trembling voice, said, "Don Guerrera you have my word..."

The Don interrupted, "Don't Don me... The only reason why I don't kill you right here, right now is because you're my fuckin brother-in-law. My taking you out would be very upsetting to my wife Catalina."

Placing his gun on Francisco's forehead, Temoc said, "Are we clear?"

Francisco seemed to be facing the wrath of a God. Perspiring from every pore, he replied with a shaken voice, "Don Guerrera for sure, *no problema...*"

Wiping the back of his neck with a handkerchief, Francisco wondered, 'Why, did I ever introduce them?'

6

A winter storm left Los Angeles with partly cloudy skies but after a day, it all had cleared, leaving the air fresh, clean, crisp and sunny.

Leon and McCooly were headed to LAX.

"Glad this nasty monsoon is over." Said Leon.

"Yeah, rare for LA."

After a few miles on Highway 10, McCooly continued, "Hey man, take this exit, La Brea South."

Fast driving Leon swirled in order to take the ramp. "What's this about?"

"I want to show you something."

At the intersection of La Brea Avenue and Don Lorenzo Drive, from the top of Baldwin Hills, they had a view of the snowcapped mountain of Big Bear ninety-eight miles away.

"I never told anyone this is where I'm going to retire," said McCooly.

"How the hell you going to do that on our salary?"

"I'm working on a plan."

"Don't get me in trouble, partner."

"During the 50's & 60's Baldwin Hills and View Park were known as the Beverly Hills for wealthy African-Americans."

"Really!?"

"Yes sir, Black Beverly Hills. During that time people of color were not permitted to purchase and own property in the affluent areas of Los Angeles. No Negroes..."

"I thought you didn't like that term?"

"That was the term used then. Prominent, wealthy doctors, dentists, entertainers... they bought lavish homes not only in View Park and Baldwin Hill but Ladera Heights as well."

"You're a cop bro' not a dentist."

"Internationally known celebrities such as Nat King Cole, Sammy Davis Jr., Sidney Poitier and Ike and Tina Turner owned extravagant homes with breathtaking views of the Los Angeles skyline."

"And neither are you an entertainer."

"Yeah, I know these places are expensive."

"What do the homes go for?"

"Starting prices in the BH community is about a million."

"What does Beverly Hills have to do with this?"

"BH, is Baldwin Hills not Beverly Hills. It's still comprised of mostly African-Americans. However, gentrification is becoming a reality."

"How so?"

"A growing influx of young whites and Asians are moving into the neighborhood. LAX International Airport being only fifteen minutes west of Baldwin Hills and freeway entrances going east, west, north and south makes it a convenient location to live. There, the hidden secret has been revealed."

Leon smiled, pleased to be listening, "How do you know all this stuff."

"It's my city, my only true love."

—

Leon and McCooly arrived late at the office of Paul Briggs, Executive Director of Aviation Flight Maintenance Services; the company that provided operations maintenance and mechanical services for most of the airlines at LAX.

Captain Robert Jenkins of the Los Angeles Airport Police was also present.

"Yes detective, Terry Mitchell was employed here for nine years." Paul Briggs answered the question Leon had posed.

"Has his behavior change lately?" Asked McCooly.

"No. Terry was a good man, a hard worker. For the life of me, I can't imagine how anything like this could happen to him and his family."

"That's the point, we're here to gather as much information as we can." Said Leon.

Captain Jenkins read from his notes: *"Terry has fulfilled all the required FAA criminal background-checks to qualify for his SIDA badge."*

"Explain SIDA," Inquired McCooly.

"Security Identification Display Area, this gives privileges to freely come and go in airport restricted areas."

"Were there any issues with substance abuse?" Asked Leon.

"He passed his entire random drug test." Interjected Paul Briggs.

"When was that?" Asked Leon.

Paul, checked Terry's file, then looked up at Leon, "Just this past July."

"Just several months ago." Said McCooly.

Leon turning to Captain Jenkins, asked, "Do you know if there were any major purchases that he might have made?"

"I don't think so but then again I didn't have daily contact with him," said the Captain, looking at Paul, he asked, "Maybe you can answer that?"

"As of now we have nothing." Paul hesitated for a second, then added, "The only one that might be of help is Frank Ruiz."

"Who is Frank?" Asked McCooly.

"He was Terry's immediate supervisor."

"We would like to speak to him after we're done here," said McCooly.

The Captain immediately answered, "He is on an extended weekend vacation."

"Returning, I believe, Wednesday morning," added Paul.

"How was the working relationship between Frank and Terry?"

"They worked well together, no issues that I am aware of," said Paul.

"I would like a list of all your employees and their job description," requested Leon.

"No problem, Human Resources will provide you with anything you might need."

Paul seemed to be in thought about something. "I recall, Terry did purchase a new truck."

"When was that?"

"A few months ago."

"What year and model?"

"A new 2018 Lincoln Navigator. I don't think it's anything because we gave out bonuses in December."

"How much was the bonus?"

"Depends on one's employment status, length of years and activity roster. The amount is anywhere from a $100.00 to $2,500.00. Depending."

"What would Terry receive?"

"Anywhere between $500-1,500."

Captain Jenkins said, "The Navigators is about sixty thousand depending on added features. I know because I am looking to purchase or lease one."

"How did he pay for it or did he take out a loan?" Asked Leon.

Paul shrugged his shoulders.

"We'll look into it." Said McCooly.

"Is there anything else?" Asked Leon.

"Can't think of anything but if I do, I'll let you know," answered Paul.

Leon asked for the contact person at the personnel office.

7

Lieutenant Rory stepped out of his office, looked around and shouted, "Leon, Cooly, I want to see you."

Once inside, Rory asked, "Leon, where are we on the missing child from the Culver City case?"

"McCooly and I have reached out to their precinct on several occasions but no response or follow-up from them."

"It's frustrating as hell." McCooly chimed in, "Their lack of cooperation. They aren't telling us anything. I don't want to, but if I have to drive over there, I will."

"LT. can you get them to at least give us a call and tell us something." Requested Leon.

"Technically it's their case. But I'll make a call or two and see what I can do."

~

The next morning at 8:00 AM, once again James and Leon were called into LT.'s office.

Leon, as soon as he walked in, thought, 'Who's this geek?'

Marcus Shaw from the North Hollywood precinct, sat crossed legged quietly looking as if he were an intellectual college professor.

Leon imagined Marcus would pull out a pipe from his pocket and start smoking at any minute.

Marcus' briefcase on the floor to his right was being protected by his left leg.

McCooly was already acquainted with Detective Shaw. He also knew that Shaw had made a reputation for himself at the Culver City Police department in the Juvenile Section.

Shaw was there to discuss the missing child case.

In the meeting, Lieutenant Rory spoke very highly of Detective Shaw. He also tried to explain the sophisticated computer-technology system Marcus had created to track down missing kids.

"I'll explain it further as we go along." Reassured Shaw.

Leon and James shared all that they had gathered.

Leon feeling confident about this new collaboration, revealed, "Terry Mitchell was employed at Los Angeles International Airport. McCooly and I interviewed Captain Robert Jenkins…"

"Detective Jenkins is he the same Jenkins from Santa Monica Airport security?" asked Marcus.

"He's at LAX now."

"I see."

"We also questioned Executive Director of Maintenance Paul Briggs. With him, we set up a time to question Frank Ruiz who is Mitchell's supervisor. He'll be back Wednesday after his extended weekend," continued Leon.

"Why don't you interview him at the house before he goes to the office," Shaw suggested.

Leon and James looked at each with a puzzled expression.

"There are small irregular deposits on Terry's bank statements but nothing significant for me to move to red flag status," said Shaw.

"I thought you are an expert on missing children?" McCooly questioned.

"Money is always at the root of all evil."

"Isn't that the truth!?" McCooly stated.

Shaw went further, "Through some computer work, I've found there is a purchase of a new SUV. He purchased it around the same time he received his annual bonus."

"Yeah, glad you're confirming this. That's what we were told." Leon said.

"What else do you guys have?" Asked Rory.

"Lucinda, Mitchell's wife, was bounced from cousins, aunts and uncles for several years after her parents were deported back to Mexico," McCooly revealed.

"Eventually she found a permanent residency with Marta and Raymundo Sanchez. She stayed with them for about four years." Said Leon.

"We found out she was an attractive young girl, well liked and had several suitors. When she met Terry

Mitchell, at age twenty, within a year they were married." Added McCooly.

"Continue with all investigation and follow-up on every single lead… Terry Mitchell, Lucinda's friends and family… don't forget anyone." Directed Rory.

In Leon's inner gut, he still had the feeling that there was something else besides checking up on these people of interest, he said, "I'll follow up on Lucinda's employment at Scenic Drive Financial."

Lieutenant Rory continued, "Marcus here, is a wizard when it comes to computers. He'll track down anything, anybody, counterfeit, fraudulent trafficking… especially if dealing with kids. I want you guys to work as a tight unit, collaborating with one another. No holding back." Rory demanded.

Outside the office, after the meeting, McCooly in a subtle voice, turned to Leon, "What the hell is this, can't we just do our job like we have done all these years?"

Leon didn't answer.

~

From the top of the cliff behind his extended property, Don Hector Guerrera and Temoc watched the sun slowly disappear in the horizon. The array of colors: yellow, red, orange on a blue skyline-canvas, made the sunset look like the work of divine intervention.

Don Hector, a desperado of venomous means, pushed Maximo, his magnificent black stallion, fast and hard. Maximo seemed to glide gracefully and effortlessly across the field as if to reach a designated destination before the sky would turn dark.

Temoc with ethereal skills as a horseman, also goaded his brown-hair Andalusian thoroughbred as he rode alongside his mentor.

Don Hector Guerrera, the mastermind and founder of the Kaliffa Cartel, ruled his Empire like a maniacal despot, extending unimaginable wealth and fortune to those in his close-inner-circle through his meticulous and detailed maneuverings, beyond their imagination. However, there was a price to be paid; dancing with the devil, one can only do in hell.

His Cartel over the years controlled extended lands in Mexico vised between his iron hands.

Don Hector had always seen California as a wide prosperous market to sell his contraband goods, especially illicit drugs. The gangs of Los Angeles played an important role in his well thought-out distribution set-up.

The two men began to descend a narrow path along the side of a steep hill. Slowing down was a precautionary measure, so as not to let their horses lose their footing.

They half-galloped their horses for another quarter of a mile before they came to an open field. Reaching the bottom of the cliff they stopped and looked as far as their eyes could see.

"You are still a good rider." Said Hector.

"You taught me well, *Padrino*."

"Out of respect you call me *Padrino* but you have always been more like a son to me."

"You took me in and treated me like family. Taught me everything I know."

"We were rotting in a jail."

"You gave me a life *Padrino*." Temoc sat tall on his horse, stroking the long neck of his pedigree. He continued, "Look at me riding this beautiful animal. You have given me money, women, plenty to eat, drink and respect. Men in our world fear you."

Hector, proud and bold, said. "Look Temoc," with stern eyes pointed at the horizon, "My law rewards the one who possess what he takes."

No more words were spoken as the two men sat quietly on top of their horses admiring the view. There was peace and calm before them.

The calm broken by Hector's edict, "*Hijo* you are a good earner that is why I am sending you back. Our distributors have gotten soft, lazy. They have become too comfortable. I need you to take control and put things in order again especially in California."

"*Si, se hace, Tio.*"

"I know you will do whatever it takes."

8

Leon and James drove through the Boyle Heights community, in an unmarked patrol car.

Everyone on the streets knew they were from the LAPD.

"This area always reminds me of my home in Cali especially on hearing the sounds of Latin music and conversation in Spanish. Do you smell it?" Asked Leon.

"I smell BBQ."

"My good friend that's the smell of *carne asada* being grilled."

James was always the co-pilot of the two, because he couldn't drive and talk at the same time. It actually had to do more with his injury he had received that night in North Carolina.

Leon not being a native of LA, would be enamored with the conversation James provided; history, stats and figures. However, on quite a few occasions including this run, Leon reminded him, "Cooly sometimes I think you forget I've lived here for more than twenty years."

"It's not the same bro', you weren't born here. Things change. As an example, Boyle Heights is a community existing on a 6.5 square mile radius with a whopping 94% Latino ratio."

"Haven't you heard, Mexico is silently taking back California," Leon laughed out loud.

James chuckled, joining his laughter.

"It's hard to believe that in the '50's this same community was racially and ethnically diverse, comprising mostly of Jews, Latinos, Blacks and Japanese-Americans."

Leon didn't say anything.

They drove down the street filled with mostly Latinos.

"What happened?" asked Leon.

"The Jews packed up and left because of the banks red-lining the neighborhood. They could. The others stayed behind because they couldn't afford to leave. Eventually Blacks moved out or were pushed out, depends to whom you talk to. The Latinos just kept on coming. There you have it - LA History 101."

"Thanks for the wisdom Professor McCooly. Here's our address, 21311 Britton Avenue."

They got out and approached the large old Victorian house, built in the early '20's. The front yard was spacious with a well-manicured lawn. The garden had red roses, barrel cactus and other desert plants evenly distributed in front of the house. A high six foot fence covered with ivy separated the side property from the neighbor's.

James made a mental note of a driver passing by, too young to be sporting a smoke-grey convertible Bentley. The driver attempted not to be conspicuous but McCooly noticed his inquisitive glances.

Leon knocked on the door of the house.

After a few moments a young Latina opened the door.

Leon introduced himself, then added, "And this is Detective James McCooly. Is Frank Ruiz home?"

The young girl turned and yelled inside the house, "*Papi* there are two detectives here to see you."

A middle aged Latino appeared.

"Mr. Ruiz?"

"What's this about?"

As they showed their badges, Leon asked, "Are you Frank Ruiz?"

"Yes."

"We are LAPD Detectives Leon Sicardo and James McCooly. May we have a word with you, sir?"

"*Papi* is this about me ditching school?"

"No *mamita*. Go inside."

The teenager relieved, immediately left.

"It is regarding Terry Mitchell." Said McCooly.

Frank made the sign of the cross. "Terry, may God have mercy. Come in."

They followed him into the living room.

Leon observed the premise and thought, 'I know at times I'm molded but this is the opposite of what I thought I would find. No pictures and statutes of the Virgin Mary holding baby Jesus. I'm surprised there aren't hanging crucifixes, neither small icons of deceased saints on the walls. No presence of the Catholic

Church's themes, usually strongly present in our Latino's cultures.'

Leon took a seat in the middle of a plush dark brown leather couch, while Frank sat across from him in a matching leather chair.

Like a ghost, invisible as the Smith & Wesson hidden inside his jacket, James positioned himself strategically by sitting comfortably on one of the leather covered bar stools by the oval shaped built-in bar at the corner of the living room. He observed the bar fully stocked with the finest liquors. He took out a pad and pen.

"How can I help? Anything for Terry." Said calmly, Frank Ruiz.

"At this juncture we're just gathering information," said James.

Frank pointed to the bar. "Can I offer you anything?"

"No thank you." Replied James.

"We're on official business," Leon responded.

"I can't believe Terry is gone."

"When did you hear about the incident?" Asked Leon.

"I got a call from the office." Answered Frank.

"Tell me what you know about Terry?"

"He was a good guy, I liked him."

"What do you mean by 'good guy'?" Asked James.

"He was easy going. He was willing to do work for people in a pinch."

"Did he have any problems at work or with anyone you know about?"

"Everyone at work liked him. Terry did his work and then went home to his family."

"You're his supervisor, right?" Asked James.

"Yes"

"Did you ever socialize with Terry or his family?" Asked Leon.

"It was strictly a working relationship."

"I understand you were gone for a few days?"

"Took a couple days off from work, after my shift Thursday evening."

"If you don't mind, where did you go?" Asked James.

"Visiting friends and family."

"Where was that?" Asked Leon.

"Mexico."

"Pretty big country. Where exactly?" Inquired Mc-Cooly.

Frank took a few moments before answering, "Playa Del Carmen."

James and Leon wrote the name down in their notepads.

"Over the last few weeks or days, did Terry act strange or unusual in any way?" Asked Leon.

Frank reflected for a moment. "No. Nothing unusual"

"Any girlfriend or mistress that you were aware of?" Asked Leon.

Frank taken back by the question, finally answered, "None that I know of."

Frank's wife came in and apologized for interrupting the conversation. With a questioning stare she looked at the detectives, then asked her husband, *"Amor, voy a la tienda, tu necesitas alguna cosita?* (Sweetheart, I am going to the store do you need anything?)

"No. Nothing *mamita*."

She leaned over and whispered in his ear, "Are we OK?"

"Humm hum."

She kissed him on both cheeks. She said her good-byes to the detectives and left through the dining room area.

As Leon followed her with his eyes, he noticed what seemed to be an original painting hanging on one of the walls.

He turned to Frank. "Is that piece from the Colombian painter?"

Without thinking, a boastful Frank, answered, "Yes It's a Carlos Ruiz?

"You're not related, are you?" asked Leon.

"No. Just similar last name." Answered Frank.

"May I see it up close? I love his work." Leon inquired.

Frank proud of his art piece, "Sure be my guest."

Leon studied for a while the intriguing art work.

"How do you know about Carlos?" Asked Frank.

"I met him several times. I have an original piece myself from him."

"I complement your taste, detective. As you know his work is not cut-rate."

"What are you saying Mr. Ruiz, a cop can't afford an expensive piece of art?" Said McCooly.

Caught off guard by the remark, Frank replied, "No. Of course not, most people aren't aware of him and if they do… can't really afford him."

"Who buys his work?" asked McCooly.

"People who enjoy the finer things in life and businessmen looking for a good investment…" Changing the subject Frank continued, "How is that you met Carlos?"

"I was on the Olympic swim team for Colombia in 1968. Carlos was commissioned to do some artwork representing our country."

Leon returned to where he was sitting and noticed on the opposing wall another Carlos Ruiz original.

Without saying a word, Frank felt he was being questioned by Leon's baffled look.

"Got it in Colombia," Frank changed the subject once again, "Are you guys familiar with the artist Vladimir Cora?

"No," said James, "Can't say that I am."

"Cora is from my country," proudly replied Frank.

"So you're from Mexico?" Leon asked.

James blurted out, "How is it that you guys are into all this stuff?"

Leon winked at Frank and replied, "We Latinos are into the beauty of our culture."

Frank took a sigh and sat comfortably in his plush chair.

"Where in Mexico are you from?" asked Leon.

"Mexico City, been here twenty five years," answered Frank.

James sat listening to their conversation, taking notes.

"I was in my teens when I came to LA. I didn't speak a word of English," continued Frank.

"Neither did I. It was tough especially throughout my schooling." Said Leon.

"Tell me about it, I struggled in high school and had to drop out of college," continued Frank.

"But you have done well. Beautiful home…" commented James.

Frank interrupted, "I believed in the American Dream."

"Frank, one more question. Do you know anyone that might have wanted Terry dead?" Asked Leon.

James observed Frank's body language, stiffening.

"No. I have no idea."

James looked at Leon, "Do you have any other questions?"

"I'm good for now."

James informed Frank that there might be more questioning in the near future.

"OK, anything… I can do to help." Frank said feeling as confident as he possibly could.

On their drive back to the precinct, James and Leon realized they were not able to put their fingers on it but something wasn't quite right.

"The house is nicely done with a modern Spanish style ambiance. I almost wanted to ask if an interior designer was involved in decorating the place." Said Leon.

"The living room and dining room had a rustic color and orange/yellow tile floors. The ceiling-to-floor wall was burnt-red while the others were off-white or beige. The trimming in natural brown teak wood was kind of pretty fancy and expensive for this neighborhood." Added McCooly.

"Yeah and all the furniture looked even more expensive. Authentic antiques, Mexican and Caribbean sculptures, neatly displayed throughout the rooms that we were able observe." Said Leon.

"That clay half-bust set on the stand…"

"And that knife with the gold-handle looked biblically ancient." Said Leon.

"I had to remind myself that I wasn't in the Latin American Museum of Modern Art." Concluded McCooly.

Leon became quiet, somber and reflective. '*My father an artist with little means of generating an income created hardships for us. Because of his inability to properly care for me and my sister, over a period of time, Mom became angry and hostile toward him. He was a true artist, he just wanted to create beauty. Barely able to provide the basics for us, he became piqued and angry with the unfair treatment he was receiving from life. And as the years passed, he took on the realities of living with more and more indignation and bitterness. He began drowning his self-pity in a bottle. Fighting between Mom and Papi became routine.*'

As Leon was growing up, he became the "man-child," the peace maker in the family. He couldn't understand how his soft spoken father, Eduardo, could be loving one moment, confrontational and wrathful the next.

Eduardo started leaning on him as if his son had understood his father's emotional problems. At that very young age the only thing that Leon understood with certainty - was confusion.

Leon became non-confrontational and did whatever necessary to make sure there was peace in the house.

OLIVER SIMS

9

The drugs and alcohol gave the group at the party a false sense of invincibility. On several couches, some were drinking and participating in an orgy of sniffing white powder, others were fondling loosely-clad *chicas*.

A mixed group ranging from Mexicans, Hondurans, to El Salvadorans were cheering Mario Lopez, himself a Mexican.

That year, Mario had proclaimed himself leader of the Height Street Ghetto Boys, boasting at being the new king on the block.

This didn't sit well with some of the hatchet men including his best friend Juan "Tequila" Pasquel.

Known as the HS Ghetto Boys, they were a small group of thugs attempting with determined brutal force to be "serious" gangsters. They were expanding and controlling the sales of narcotics within a ten block radius in the Boyle Heights community.

The participants were mostly in their late twenties and some in their early thirties.

Mario unrestrained was talking loud and being obnoxious. He was high and hyped from the evening by his own self-proclaimed power. Completely drunk.

Fueled by pure uncut cocaine, he had become heinous, completely disheveled and his face reflected the hard street life of a gangster making him look much older than twenty eight.

An inebriated nineteen year old girl stumbled, knocking over a tray full of coke. The guys yelled as if the worst disaster had just happened. Pico Rivera, her boyfriend, livid, stood up striking her face, knocking her to the floor.

"What the...? You stupid bitch!"

Mario, even though high, grabbed Pico's arm. "Be cool *amigo*. There is plenty of *cocaína* to go around."

Pico still angry, "Bitch scoop it up."

With a back-hand slap, he knocked her down again.

Mario grabbed Pico by the throat, "Armando hosted the party and if he found out about this, he would turn in his grave."

He pushed Pico away and broke out laughing uncontrollably.

Mario loose-lipped revealed that the day before he had snuffed Armando.

Armando Vázquez a drug kingpin responsible for trafficking in the region for Don Hector Guerrera never accepted Mario as a true Mafioso. He always considered Mario just a common desperado. On one occasion Armando completely shamefaced Mario in front of his homeboys by calling him a "*pinche culero.*"

Juan "Tequila" turned to Mario, wide eyed, "Shut the fuck-up man, are you f... crazy?"

"What? I ain't scared of nobody. I'll shoot whoever the fuck gets in my way." He then pulled out a gun from behind the back of his jeans, "I'm the mother-fuc... man around here." Mario said still in a bravado voice.

Several girls screamed ducking for cover.

The room became quiet, filling with a palpable tension.

All eyes were on Mario.

The smell of fear permeated the room.

Mario looked around and pointed the gun at no one in specific. Seeing he had everyone's attention, once again he tucked the gun behind the back of his pants. He broke out hysterically laughing.

Everyone began laughing, trying to ease their own anxiety.

The party continued.

The only one not laughing was Juan "Tequila." He looked at Mario concerned, "You are one *loco* son of a bitch."

"This is where we make our bones. We go back to Tijuana days. Now let's get ready *mi amigo* to grow our own business."

"I got your back."

Both swigged from a shared bottle of Padron Tequila.

Maricela Barrone sat in a corner, on the arm of a tattered leather couch. She took several drags from a cigarette made of Humboldt's finest marijuana plant.

She smoked it to calm her nerves, while watching Mario with disdained eyes. Deep down, she was placating a desire that was boiling inside her, to take revenge on him with the P-32 handgun she had hidden in her purse.

In the years as the mistress of Armando Vázquez, she had always been instructed, by him, not to ever show any emotions when dealing with "business."

To lay low, observe, listen and act as if enjoying oneself no matter what the occasion, this time it would be no different wanting to take care of Mario.

Pico Rivera, mumbled to Juan "Tequila" and Mario, "I like how you guys do business."

"Right now just sit back and party," said Mario.

Pico who felt left out, said, "What's our next move?"

"We'll talk later after some of these fools are gone." Said Mario in a low voice.

～

3:00 AM.

Most of the gang members and their *hiñas* were strewn throughout the apartment. Some sleeping on the floor, others slouched in chairs or couches snoring like a choir out of tune.

Tequila had left the party and Pico after a few minutes did the same.

One gang member, sleeping on the kitchen table, was out cold holding to his beer bottle as if his life depended on it.

Mario was sound asleep with one of his many women in the second bedroom down the hall.

Maricela pretended to have fallen asleep, kept squinting her eyes to see if everyone had passed-out.

Sitting next to her, she found herself with a guy's head leaning on her shoulder. He was motionless as if he had been knocked out by the undisputed champion, Manny Pacquiao. She slowly slithered from under the man's head, making sure not to wake him.

She looked around taking inventory of the individuals in the room. On tip toes, meticulously and slowly she crept down the hallway. Peeking in the first room, she didn't recognize the couple sleeping. She was looking for Mario.

At the next bedroom she gently turned the doorknob, softly, making sure it didn't squeak. She peeked inside.

Mario and the woman next to him seemed to be in deep sleep.

She then back peddled to the main room.

Maricela unlatched the lock to the entrance of the front door, she then left the house as she tucked her purse under her arm. Making sure no one was nearby, she looked right, then left.

She made sure to see that the black SUV was parked down the street.

In quick steps she made her way towards it. The dark tinted window on the driver side, rolled down.

Maricela leaned her head inside; she heard a baritone voice from the back seat, "Where is he?"

"Sleeping in the second bedroom."

"*Querida*, you did well." Said the voice.

The driver, as soon as he was tapped on his shoulder by the person seating in the back, handed Maricela a wad of rolled one-hundred dollars bills wrapped with a rubber band.

The voice continued, "That should help you and my godchild."

Maricela looked at the wad of money and tucked it in her purse as if it were the normal thing to do.

In appreciation, she said, "*Mucha gracias.*"

No answer from the back seat.

The car window rolled up.

Maricela returned to her own car parked a block away.

"Get ready," the voice instructed to the men in the car.

Dressed in dark clothes, they exited the SUV, holding semi-automatic handguns with silencers.

The voice continued, "Boys... he's mine..."

At the house, one of the men easily opened the unlatched door left by Maricela. They stepped into the living room.

Instructions, from the baritone voice, intended for one of the henchmen, "Stay here... shoot anyone who stirs."

They walked down the hall to the first bedroom, a few seconds later, they heard coming from the living room, "No, don't..." It was a scream of fear.

Then the faint noise of a gun silencer, the sound of thick glass of a coffee-table shattering and a hard loud thumping sound of a limp body hitting the floor.

One of the henchmen opened the first bedroom door. A startled young woman, saw the two men standing in the doorway, jumped out of bed. Using a pillow to cover her naked body, she was shot point black as she attempted to get up. A second bullet entered her forehead.

Two other shots were fired, hitting the person who was still in bed; leaving the sheets soaked in red.

As each person woke up, the gunman in the living room made sure everyone received at least one bullet to the head. Quickly, silently and deadly.

In the second bedroom, two men stood in the doorway. The woman next to Mario screamed as she attempted to find cover. Her squawking was quieted by a single bullet.

Mario woke up from the commotion. Still dazed and confused from the drugs and alcohol, he sat at the edge of the bed, butt naked, attempted to reach for his gun, on top of the dresser near him.

The two guys were pointing their guns at him.

"Who the fuck are you?" Mario asked angrily.

The voice replied, "Think of me as Lucifer?"

Mario looked at him, speechless. Fear, forced him to come to his senses.

"I came for your soul… Mario," said the voice.

"I haven't done anything."

"Really? What do you think brings us to this place, at this very moment?" asked the voice.

"Whatever it is I can fix it," pleaded Mario.

"It's too late 'Sissy.'"

Mario's anger welled up. "I shot the last man who called me that."

"Exactly," said the voice.

Mario angrier and in a total state of despair, shouted again, "Who the fuck are you?"

"This is who I am." The man pulled out an eagle's claw and with his right hand slashed it into Mario's chest; the talons dug deep clasping at his heart. He then pulled the trigger with his left finger. Mario's skull was pierced by a bullet between his eyes.

He didn't hear, "Goodbye... Mario."

~

Maricela sat on the couch in her two bedroom lavishly furnished apartment, affectionately caressing her baby. She stared at him with the overwhelming love a mother could have for her first born.

Cupping her breast, she felt him hungrily suckle on her nipple.

"That's right my child, eat so you can be big and strong." She said lovingly.

In a tender hush toned voice she sang a song, the same lullaby her mother had sung to her as a child in Vera Cruz, Mexico.

Montebello, California was her home now. The turmoil of how to provide for her infant son had become a heavy burden for her. In these past few days, she was conflicted with the thought whether to stay or return to Mexico.

Armando Vásquez, her lover had been the provider and father of her child.

Now he was gone.

She knew Armando had loved her, even though the rules of gangster life would never allow for a self-made-man within the Cartel to divorce his spouse. She knew the rules of the streets and had also accepted the life of a mistress.

Across from her, sat comfortably in a chair with his legs crossed an attractive physically built man in his thirties, sipping on a beer. The tattoos on his hands and up his arms looked menacing and frightening; to some people, it was attractive and to others, considered even a work of art. The Twin Towers tattoo on his left bicep was the mark of survival from Folsom Prison.

He was watching Maricela with adoration as she attended to her son.

"You have adapted well to motherhood."

"Thank you, *Pappi*. At first I thought it was a mistake but Armando would always say, 'Everything happens for a reason.' I may no longer be with him but I did have our son. How am I going to take care of my child without Armando?" She lowered her head in pain, then looked up at Temoc. "I loved Armando. That piece of shit Mario took him away from me... from us... I'm glad that little *puta* is dead."

"You got your revenge. Armando was loyal, a good earner. We take care of our own... of our *familia*. We'll work something out for you. Don't worry," reassured Temoc.

He went over to Maricela and gently took the child in his arms and cradled him like a loving father. Temoc caressed his godchild then kissed him on both cheeks.

He looked at the infant tenderheartedly.

～

The cell phone rang intruding Leon's sleep.

Startled, 'That damn dream again! Woods... Running... Sophia... Catching my breath... breathing hard. Once again running. A dive into the river.'

In bed that morning, with eyes semi closed, he looked at the clock on the nightstand, 4:41.

'Dam phone.' He answered.

He heard, "Wake up pretty boy."

"Couldn't it wait until 6:00?"

"The early bird catches the assholes."

"I don't crack heads this early."

"Leon! He struck again."

"I'm putting on pants as we speak."

"I'll be at your place in fifteen minutes."

"Cooly, I'll meet you downstairs."

In less than fifteen minutes James had arrived.

As soon as Leon sat in the passenger seat, James handed him a cup of coffee.

"Cooly, don't you ever sleep?"

"Not a decent night since Nam."

Leon took a sip, appreciating McCooly's kind gesture.

"How do we know it's him?" Asked Leon.

"The claw to the heart and the nine millimeter... to the forehead."

~

Once they arrived in the neighborhood, James commented, "Look at them, typical residents of Boyle Heights peering out the windows. Fearful of getting involved, satisfied just to watch all the commotion that go on around them."

A TV-news van arrived.

"Now the real show begins," laughed McCooly.

Yolanda Martinez, an attractive, headstrong, confident LA Police Officer was the first on the scene but the ghoulish killings left her nauseated. Not the way she had planned to start the day.

"You look a little pale," said McCooly

"Detectives, I've never seen anything like this."

They walked into the house, the smell of wine, tequila, weed, stale cigarettes... Vomit. All... permeated throughout the house.

Carnage... everywhere.

"Something of interest in the other room," said Yolanda, as she walked towards it.

James and Leon followed, passing the first bedroom where two bodies laid lifeless on a bed soaked with blood.

James and Leon were already wearing latex gloves.

As they were about to enter the second room, Officer Martinez stopped in her tracks, outside the door.

James and Leon stepped in the room.

"This is a real massacre," James said looking at Officer Martinez.

"There doesn't seem to be any forced entry. But there is something else..." she said.

They entered the bedroom, the smell of acrid urine and blood was overbearing.

James kneeled and with his gloved hand, examined Mario's head wound. Looking up at both officers, he said, "No real evidence of a fight or struggle."

Leon leaned forward to examine the woman, near the door, lying down, face up. "Shot point blank."

Officer Martinez pointed to the dead Hispanic man, "Detectives, meet Mario Lopez."

"You know this guy?" asked Leon.

"He was an up and coming street thug from the Height Street Ghetto Boys a/k/a HS Ghetto Boys," said Officer Martinez.

"Yeah, he was a low life pinched for drug possession, attempted robbery, assault, you know, the typical MO for a want-to-be gangster."

"He is the son of Baca Lopez a career criminal from Mexico. When I worked patrol, I busted the old man on several occasions. Now he's doing twenty to life at Folsom Prison," said Leon.

"Like father like son," added McCooly.

"There are connections between the murders in Culver City and here in Boyle Heights," said Leon.

"Two drastically different communities, with diverse demographics, yet crime scenes are similar," said McCooly.

"So, the killer here, is most likely the same murderer as the one in Culver City?" Officer Martinez surprisingly asked.

"I believe so," answered Leon.

"Who and why would anyone murder a family across town then turn around and massacre a group of party people?" asked Martinez.

"It's drug related. A mess like this is almost always related to narcotics." Added McCooly.

"All slaughtered and executed gangster style," added Officer Martinez.

"Smells like a Cartel," said James.

"Can't waste any time. Start questioning the neighbors," instructed Leon.

"Did," confirmed Yolanda.

"And…?"

"No results… too early, besides no one will talk."

"The only thing you're going to get in this neighborhood is *omertá*," said James.

~

At the corner diner, officers Martinez, Leon and McCooly took a break from the horrific "massacre."

The adrenaline was still rushing through everyone's veins.

Over a cup of coffee Officer Martinez was reading in sotto voce what she had written: "*Found a young Latina lying in the bed with a sheet covering her body up to her neck. It seemed she was caught by surprise. A single bullet lodged in the middle of her forehead. A Hispanic male, found on his back, naked next to the young woman's body, with gunshot wounds from projectiles, 9mm. To his chest... a marking on the left side of his chest, over his heart. Per detectives on the scene, McCooly and Sicardo, assume that they are the same type of gash wounds found on the victim at the Culver City murders.*"

"We'll have the forensics at LAPD confirm if the markings are from the claw of the same predator bird," Leon added in a soft voice and visibly shaken.

"Come on Leon!" McCooly said agitated, then continued quietly, "The spacing and patterns of the lines on the murder victim's chest are from the claw of an eagle... most likely that of a Bald eagle."

They left the diner in a solemn mood. Barely saying another word as they returned to the precinct.

Each one dealt with what they had seen in their own private way.

10

Hard-pounding-knocks on the front door, an excited loud voice yelled, "Juan wake up."

"Tequila get your ass up," another distraught voice hollered, followed by repeated banging on the door.

"Wake up!"

Juan Tequila startled, awoke from a deep sleep, confused and disoriented from his hangover, jumped out of bed and rushed in the direction of the ruckus, nearly tripping over his own feet. Reaching the front door, he leaned over squinting with one eye and looked through the peep hole, on seeing Diego and his brother, known as Bulldog, he opened. The two guys scurried in the apartment and quickly closed the door behind them.

Bulldog shrieked, "Turn on the TV."

"What the fuck is wrong with you guys?" bellowed Juan.

"Turn on the fuckin' news, they're all dead." Diego hollered back as he pointed at the TV.

"What the hell you talking about?"

"Mario and everyone in the house... dead... shot... killed...." Diego blurted out in disbelief.

Juan rubbed his eyes still trying to wake up. He scanned the living room frantically looking for the remote. On finding it, he began to surf the channels for a news station.

"What the fuck...?" Tequila demanded in an angry voice.

As Diego began to explain what had happened, the broadcaster announced: *"Following up on our earlier Breaking News of the gangland shooting in South Los Angeles, our CBS local news team is on location. We are confirming eight people were shot and killed in the early hours this morning. The police is not releasing any other information at this time. But our correspondent on the scene reported it might be a massacre related to gang drug violence. Currently there are no known survivors or witnesses. We are seeking your help, if you have any information please call the local authorities or the following toll free number appearing on the screen. All calls will be kept confidential. We will keep you informed with more details as it arrives."*

Tequila still in an induced drug fog, slowly became aware that the Mexican Mafia had murdered his friends. He had warned Mario not to ever mess with Armando. This time not only had Mario stolen Armando's drugs and money but had actually killed him. He had crossed the line. Armando was seen as a "Made Man" by the cartel. Mario's murder was a legitimate retaliation in their eyes.

"Get the fuck out of here. You know they'll be looking... you're next. You were Mario's right hand man," Bulldog warned him.

"I'll go to Mexico," immediately responded Juan Tequila.

"Are you *loco*, you can't go anywhere in Mexico that's their territory. It's like walking right in their hands," cautioned Diego.

"Go up North, to Fresno or Chico," suggested Bulldog.

"No Homey, you got to get out of the state... like to Denver or Oregon. That's it, Oregon!" He looked at Tequila with deep concern then continued, "I have *familia* working in construction there, but you can't tell them anything about all this. I'll get things set up. You have money?"

"Yeah some cocaine stashed away but not here."

"No fucking time to waste or you'll end up just like Mario."

~

At his grandmother's house, Tequila felt safe. He retrieved his cash, a good amount of heroin and coke to sell whenever he'd need more money.

Grandma, even though old and with the beginning of dementia, asked her favorite grandson, "*Chichito*, you're not in trouble again?"

"Don't worry *abuelita*, it's all good," he gave her a kiss on her forehead.

Tequila stepped out the front door, looked around and seeing the coast clear, he hurriedly walked to his car.

'It might not be so bad living in Oregon,' he thought.

He had heard some say that it was pretty country up there.

'Getting out of LA could be a good thing and a fresh start. I'd have to miss Mario's and the others' funerals.'

"Sorry Mario." He said out loud, making the sign of the cross.

He took a last look over his shoulders and quickly slithered in his car. Once inside he took a visual inspection then looked in the rear view mirror; seeing no one, took off in a hurry.

A massive sigh of relief when he saw the indication to Highway 660. At the octagonal red sign he stopped then proceeded to enter the ramp. A Ram truck traveling at high speed blind-sided him. Juan's car was crushed between the truck and a telephone pole.

The air bag deployed. Tequila was knocked unconscious.

The truck driver quickly backed up, then shifted into drive and sped off.

A black van pulled next to the crushed car; three men jumped out. One, with a crowbar wrenched open the driver's side door. The other two, pulled Juan's limp body out of the wreck. They heaved him in the van and sped off just as swiftly as they had arrived. Before anyone in the surrounding area could see what had taken place; the black van had disappeared like a ghost into the night.

~

The afternoon sun shimmered a silver sheen on the Pacific. The water's surface looked tranquil but the undercurrents were tugging. Only courageous or insane surfers in their wet suits entered the 59.54 degrees water.

Unbeknown to Leon, a woman at the end of the pier was watching him swim in that extremely cold water.

His strokes were rhythmic, precise and graceful. The right arm straight while his hand acted like a paddle as it came up through the water and extended over his head, then reentering the water. His strokes were fluid yet powerful as he swam through the challenging surf.

Leon emerged from the ocean's waters, took off his goggles and walked towards where he had left his gym bag and towel on the beach.

He noticed the woman walking barefoot toward him. In one hand she was carrying a lunch-size brown paper bag and in the other her shoes.

He removed his swimming cap, picked up his towel and dried his face. Leon squinted attempting to focus; to identify who she could be.

From a distance, she said, "Thought you could use a hot cup of coffee."

He was surprised. It was Vanessa Compose.

"What brings you here?"

"When you didn't answer your cell, I took the liberty of calling your office."

"I see."

"Your partner told me, to come to the Santa Monica pier and look for the only 'fool' swimming in the middle of the Pacific Ocean."

"Is that what he said!?"

"Yes, and also to look for a bright orange swim cap bobbing up and down in the water."

"My man James."

"He's been very resourceful for me."

"And how is that?"

"That when things get really heinous and ugly for you, you come out here. That, when you're hunting for the beast, you go swimming with the sharks to subdue your fears."

"Yeah, but he wouldn't have any of this."

"Got to admit, swimming with sharks... you have to be pretty crazy..."

"Keeps me fit... there's a rhythm to my thinking... Salt water and the flow of the currents invigorate me."

"And what about the sharks?"

"What about them?"

"Aren't you afraid?"

"I'm a cop, I have protection," pointing to the knife strapped to the lower part of his calf. "Swimming with sharks keeps me sharp and alert. I rather take my chances and swim with carnivorous fish than enter a house not knowing if there is a cold blooded killer inside ready to blow my brains out. Enough about fish. What..."

"Had to go to a funeral and didn't want to go to the studio." She interrupted.

"I am sorry about your loss."

"They're in a peaceful place now..."

They stayed silent for a few awkward minutes.

"How about sushi?"

"Not much of a sushi kind of girl but I could learn to acquire a taste for it."

"I'll introduce you to the food of the gods."

"You like it that much?"

"It's heaven…"

"Got the day off."

"Great!"

As he picking up the duffel bag, Leon's cell phone rang.

He hurriedly unzipped the bag and answered. *"Que pasa…?"* He turned away to listen. "Yeah, OK, got it. On my way."

He turned to Vanessa, "Sorry, that was 'our boy.' I gotta go. Can we talk later?"

"That's OK." She said, disappointed.

"Welcome to my life."

"I understand."

"At times it has no rhyme or reason."

"Not a 9 to 5 job. I get it."

"Where's your car?"

She pointed to the parking lot.

~

Walking across the tiny rocks and sand, reminded him of Cali, Colombia, when he had celebrated his thirteenth birthday.

'What a great time with pals, Pelajito and Machete.'

They had played a fierce and competitive soccer game. After they won their "imaginary" World Cup Championship, they snuck beer from his father's stash. At that age this was the best way to celebrate.

He felt his heart beating thunderously. He remembered: '*Running as fast as my legs would carry me. The rays of sun broke through the thick foliage. Sweat dripping from my forehead burned in my eyes, making it difficult to see. The sounds of boots right behind me. "I can make it." I kept repeating it like a mantra. "So-phia..." The branches gashed my arms and legs as I dashed through the jungle. There it was. The mountain run-off, into the River Pance, that time of year made the water flow like a jet stream. I dove in as I heard the thunder of a rifle shot. I could feel the tiny rocks, pebbles beneath my feet. When I reemerged, I swam hell-bent to save my life.'*

~

In an isolated empty warehouse in the meat-packing district in East LA, Juan Tequila was slumped semi-conscious over a chair, with hands tied behind his back. He could feel the blindfold squeezing tightly around his temples making it impossible to figure out where he was.

He was surrounded by two heavily armed, tattooed, Mexican gangsters. From buckets filled with water, two other men took turns slowly pouring water over the burlap hood that covered Tequila's face.

Tequila coughing. Chocking.

Across at the other end of the room on a sturdy wooden crate, sat Temoc. He signaled to one of the men to remove the hood. He motioned once again and the blindfold was removed as well.

Juan was totally disoriented and in no time, his fears quickly surfaced, wrenching his gut.

"Did you have a good nap?"

"Who are you...?" Asked Tequila trying to sound tough.

"Your friend Mario asked the same question."

"Huhhh!?"

There was silence.

Tequila was desperately trying to make sense of it all.

Temoc looked at him up and down, "Who am I? Let's see. My *familia* know me as Cuauhtémoc 'Temoc' Gutierrez. To my enemies I'm, 'The Archangel.'"

A chill shot through Juan's spine. Between his fear and pride, he shouted back, "If you're gonna kill me, get on with it."

"What's the hurry?"

"I told him, he was stupid for jacking you guys up."

"You guys...? What guys?"

"Kaliffa Cartel."

"What do you know about that?"

"Armando was 'A made-guy.'"

Temoc was quiet, listening.

"I wanted to work with Armando."

"Really?"

"I asked Armando for permissions to work under him. Mario was the asshole who wanted him dead."

"He laughed at us as if we were punks. He only employed real brothers, real *carnal*. Mario got pissed off. Told me, 'I'll show him who's a real gangsta.'"

"Then what?"

"A couple of days later Mario comes to me with several kilos of cocaine and heroin to sell. When I asked where it came from, he told me. Armando would set us up in business. It wasn't until later in the evening, when we were getting high that he told me he'd ambushed Armando. I told him... he was a fucking fool... I told him that now: you, me... we're all dead."

"You are wise Juan. It's come true. Everyone is dead."

"Temoc…"

"You don't have the privilege… to call me that."

"I'm begging you!"

Temoc took out a gun from his back holster.

Juan squirming, "I am a good earner. I was the one running things. Mario was the front man, only because he had good connects and a big mouth."

Temoc stood up and held the gun to Tequila's forehead.

"Give me a reason…"

"You gonna need someone to fill in for Armando. Me and my crew can do it. Why stop the flow of business? I'll run these fuckin' streets for you." Said Tequila, scared shit.

Silence. Even a rat would not have moved, making sure, not to eek a sound.

Temoc signaled with his hand to one of the men.

The man quickly exited.

"Please give me a chance." Juan Tequila pleaded again.

After a few minutes the man returned. Behind him, the clicking sound of a woman's high heels echoed off the concrete floor.

Juan Tequila was shocked.

Maricela walked over to Temoc and kissed him on his cheek. *"Hola papi."*

Tequila tensed up.

She turned to face Juan, then looked back at Temoc for instructions, "Now what?"

Temoc, slowly walked in circles around Juan, looking at him as if he was searching for something, "Do I put you to sleep or do I let you live?"

"Let him earn his bones?" Suggested Maricela.

Temoc turned to Maricela with piercing eyes filled with venom, "If he fails, you both go down."

"We can handle it." Staring at Juan, she said. "We take over the Height Street Boys and my Armando's territory and expand the business."

"Not so fast, *chica*. Only I decide who gets to live."

Gazing down in Juan's eyes, "Only if you kill the leader of the Riverside gang, Paulo DeSilva. He's a snake in the grass. He must pay taxes like everyone. Cut off the head of the snake and the others will follow. If you fail, you will never see the bullet enter the front of your head. Do you understand?"

Juan Tequila nodded.

"I didn't hear you," demanded Temoc.

"Yes, I understand," Juan said with a tremble in his voice.

"Cut him loose," Temoc signaled to one man, who was standing nearby.

Temoc looked at Maricela then at Juan, "She finds value in keeping you alive. Don't make her wrong."

"My word is good."

"Have you ever killed anyone?"

Juan remained silent.

Temoc, looking at him with the same venom as before, "Either you have or you haven't."

Juan swallowed deeply.

~

Later that evening, Maricela slowly paced from the dining room to the kitchen holding her child who was screaming earsplitting cries of discomfort. Turning to Temoc she said, "He's teething."

Temoc gently took the child from her arms. He caressed him and in a sooth gentle baritone voice, said, "Poor little *papi*to don't cry."

"You have a way with him."

"Why do you look surprised?"

"I've never seen this side of you before."

He looked at the child with tender eyes then said, "He's my *ahijado*... my godson. Hush now, don't cry little *papito*"

Temoc cradled the child in his arms and walked the floor until the room was silent. In a gentle motion he gave the infant back to Maricela.

She placed the child in the crib.

"You need to step up, work the machinery; you know how we do it."

"*Si* Temoc."

"'Cause right after Juan snuffs out Paulo, he'll have to vacate the premises. We have resources everywhere. When things die down we'll bring him back."

"How long will he be gone?"

Temoc didn't answer.

Maricela slowly rocked the little one in his cradle.

11

On a large white board in the conference room at the Hollenbeck precinct were two distinct columns written in large capital letters:

CULVER CITY HOMICIDES
Terry Mitchell – vic
Lucinda Morales-Mitchell (Wife) – vic
Teenage daughter – vic
Missing child – ?
Terry's boss – further questioning
Airport security – further questioning
Apache's markings – common denominator

Under the other column:

BOYLE HEIGHTS HOMICIDES.
Mario – vic

Seven individuals at party crime scene – vics
Apache's markings – common denominator

Leon and McCooly were reviewing the names.

"We should also start adding dates, times and any other related information," said McCooly.

"What do we have from forensic?" Inquired Leon.

"Not much."

"Come on Cooly work your magic with Diane."

"Even if she is Head of Forensic, stuff takes time to cook."

"Cooly, write next to Mitchell's wife - that she is from Mexico."

Leon staring at the name, *Apache*, continued, "The hell with Mexico, who is this son of a bitch, instead!?"

"He clawed Synque Rodrigues two years ago…"

"With his damn eagle markings… he's back."

McCooly went to the board picked up a black marker wrote in bold large letters: *DRUG CONNECTION!* Then said, "I want this asshole."

Leon walked towards the door.

"Where you going bro'?" asked Cooly.

Leon walked out without giving an answer.

~

Leon made his way to the smoking lounge, a patrolman who was leaving the area acknowledged Leon by tipping his hat, "Detective."

Leon sat back in a chair on the patio. He pulled out a petite Romeo Y Julieta, one of Cuba's finest; lit it, took a drag savoring the taste and exhaled.

The air was still. No wind. Quiet.

He found himself alone thinking: '*The eyes of the FARC commanders, for different reasons, were focused on me and my father. He was a quite soft spoken artist but had become an outspoken opponent against the military leaders. At first, FARC officials considered my father just a drunk. It was when he was sober and rational that they became irritated and concerned. His sharp tongue, wit and intellect were disturbing factors for the leaders. During the same time, they targeted me as a possible youthful recruit. I was fourteen when FARC officers had a glimmer in their eye toward me. My athletic, strong-willed character was well liked in the community. Given the right training, develop in me the correct discipline, I could lead and attract others to join the movement. For young boys in dysfunctional families living in poverty, the Revolution Armed Forces of Colombia was becoming a means to survival. My father would hear nothing of this. He was protective of me and wanted me to have nothing to do with FARC. My eyes at that time were only on Sophia.*'

~

A few minutes after Leon had left Cooly, Officer Yolanda Martinez entered the conference room.

"Detective McCooly, didn't mean to disturb you."

"No problem, what's up Sargent?"

"I want to run something by you."

He pulled a chair for her to sit.

"One of my informants heard about a large shipment of heroin."

"Really?"

"Don't have all the details yet."

"What do ya' got then?"

"He said something about a house cleaning going on."

"What do you mean?"

"Something about, before the drugs hit the streets..."

Cooly gave her a questioning look.

"I'm sure it has to do with the rash of recent killings."

Leon returned from his smoke.

McCooly immediately said, "She's just informing me... There's a shipment of drugs coming in."

"We can share this with LT."

Officer Yolanda and McCooly gave each other a high-five.

Keep me posted on anything no matter how small or insignificant it may seem," said Cooly.

"Will do." Responded Officer Martinez.

12

Marcus Shaw, was already in Lieutenant Peter Rory's office when James and Leon walked in.

Shaw greeted them.

"Good to see you," answered Leon.

"Officer Shaw, here, has some news," said LT.

"Any info at all, can go a long way," added Mc-Cooly.

"Tell them what you've already told me."

"We've gathered some intelligence on a possible children smuggling ring," explained Detective Shaw.

"You got my undivided attention," answered Leon.

"Yeah!" added McCooly.

"As you know we're working closely with local FBI agents on the Mitchell case in Culver City. We apprehended an illegal immigrant on a drug bust yesterday. He wants to co-op a deal, in exchange, he wants for his two kids born here in LA to remain with their mother."

"What does Immigration and Customs Enforcement has to say about a deal with an illegal?" asked Leon.

"ICE will cooperate only if they see a win for their department."

"OK, how does it tie in to the Mitchell's case?" asked McCooly.

"Our recent incarcerated dealer claims that Terry Mitchell stole drugs from a Mexican cartel and attemptted to sell it on the open market."

"Let me guess," interrupted McCooly.

"He claims that the cartel only received a third of the expected street value," answered Shaw.

"So by the time the Cartel caught up to him..." LT. added.

"He had spent most of the money and couldn't pay the full value back," interrupted Shaw.

"How did Terry get his hands on their drugs?" LT. asked.

"We don't know, but it seems as usual, an amateur trying to play outside his league," commented Detective Shaw.

"Give 10 points to Team Mexico and zero for Team Mitchell," said McCooly smiling.

"I'm taking all this with a grain of salt." Said Shaw.

"And the missing child?" inquired Leon.

"There are several leads we're investigating. The strongest intel may unfortunately take us to Mexico."

"That's a scary thought," commented Leon.

"God have mercy... not Mexico," McCooly responded.

"They just haven't cooperated the way we've wanted in the past," said Detective Shaw.

"Tell me about it," LT. confirmed.

"We've looked at the street surveillance camera from Mitchell's next door neighbor. It shows images of a parked car and what looks like two Latino males walking in the direction of his home. We can't see their faces clearly but..."

"How do we know they're Latino?" McCooly inquired.

"It's a guess based on how they're dressed," acknowledged Detective Shaw.

"You're telling us, your hunch is based on racial profiling?" Questioned McCooly.

"If they dress like one and have the swagger of a gang banger, the likelihood is, they're probably a Mexican a/k/a, *cholo*," remarked LT. Rory.

"Call it what you like LT., but racial profiling is not the answer," said McCooly pissed off.

"Gentlemen, gentlemen... this is all we've got right now," said Shaw.

"We're already doing the heavy work," said Leon.

"We work well as a team," replied LT., then continued looking at Shaw, "Is there anything else? If not we're done for today."

Leon's cell buzzed. "I need to take the call." He stepped out to answer.

~

"Are you still on duty?"

"Why?" asked Leon.

"I need a drink."

"Martini... two olives?"

"One should never ask a lady to drink alone."

"Had a hard day?"

"Probably not as hard as yours."

Leon smiled. "Same place?"

"Meet you in an hour."

~

At Eddie Cole's, Leon sat sipping his bourbon on-the-rocks and as he had done many other times before admired on the side wall the large 50" x 55" oil painting by the African-born visual artist Emmy Lu.

This work on canvas, titled *"Precious,"* in a gold and infused bronze metal frame, was that of an elegantly poised woman with dark complexion sitting in a chair exposing her contours. Her shoulder-length black hair weaved in dreadlocks was intertwined with strips of gold cloth, wearing a multiple strands of turquoise and small white-seashells neckless. She had a look of grace and dignity in her vibrant burgundy red dress.

First time visitors and regulars alike would be transfixed and mesmerized by the beauty of Emmy Lu's artwork.

Leon found himself in very deep thoughts as he continued sipping his Four Roses.

Leon had learned to control and shut down his emotions and feelings, both in his family and dealing with outsiders. Even at a young age he felt it was his responsibility to protect his family. Through it all, he maintained a close bond and relished some of the fond memories of his father. *'One night while helping my intoxicated father to bed, I took to heart my father's words, "Son never forget that your name is strong. A lion is king of all the beasts, he fears no other animal. You are a lion, fear no man and protect your family. Don't grow up and become a dreamer like me."'*

But then there were others, which were more quarrelsome. *'I never saw the blow coming, my father struck me down. My lip bleeding, I picked myself up off the floor ready to retaliate but my father had already passed-out on the bed. I also loved and had great affecttion toward my mother but even this was met with mixed emotions. I desired to be close to her but I could never vanquish the stories surrounding her. I lost the trust, a son might have for his mother.'*

He couldn't understand why he'd remembered this one particular day: *'I was agitated that day, I knelt on the pew next to my mother. Staring at a dying Jesus on the cross, I turned and whispered to her, "Why do I have to do this?"*

"To confess your sins."

"I'm just a kid."

"Everybody is born into this world with sin."

"I told all of mine to the good father the last time."

"All boys have sins. Now be quite and say your prayers."

"I'll wait until the priest tells me how many Hail Mary's and Our Father's, I have to say."

On entering the confessional booth always reminded Leon of sitting in a puny dark closet. As he knelt down he heard the priest slide to the side the small screen door revealing the shadow of his profile.

Ten year old, Leon Sicardo made the sign of the cross: *"Bless me father, I don't have any sins to tell."*

"It's been about two weeks since we last spoke, Leon. Have you seen the girl you spoke about, in our previous conversation?"

"Yes."

"And what about those impure thoughts we discussed?"

"My conscience is clean, father."

"Are you still caring for your papa*?"*

"Yes, even when he drinks too much."

"Is there anything else?"

"No."

"Stay away from the girls, they will lead you to sin and the hells of fire. Say twenty five Hail Mary's and twenty Our Father's."

"Why so many prayers."

'For your protection my son."

"Protection from what?"

"Sins of the flesh."'

Thinking that the hearsay and rumors had been haunting him ever since... just like the thought of Sophia... throughout his life.

The faint yet profoundly exquisite aroma of Chanel Coco Noir, brought him out of his reveries.

As he saw Vanessa approach, the thought, 'I should be working on the multiple unsolved cases. Instead here I am, waiting for this woman. But a man's got to eat.'

Before Leon could fasten the middle button on his suit jacket, to stand and greet her, Vanessa leaned over and smacked a kiss on his cheek.

She was surprised to see a Grey Goose vodka-martini with two olives already ordered for her. She smiled.

"Need a sympathetic ear?"

Vanessa didn't answer but threw back her drink.

~

Juan Tequila and Maricela had called a meeting with Juan's boys.

Sitting around the table at Maricela's kitchen, Juan Tequila, Pico Rivera, Diego and Bulldog were serving themselves portions of tacos, refried beans, yucca and salad.

She placed another fresh cold bottle of Patrón on the table.

Juan immediately took a swig directly from the bottle.

Pico lit a joint.

"Boys don't get too fucked up."

"Come on *Momi* we're having a little fun, he ain't dead or nothing," Bulldog laughed.

"Fuck you man! We got business to discuss," said Juan.

Everyone laughed out loud.

"Pass the blunt. Asshole," demanded Diego.

"Why I'm alive is due to the grace of God," Juan Tequila looked at Maricela, "If it weren't for her…"

Everyone lifted their drinks and saluted Maricela.

~

Leon and Vanessa were just about to start in earnest their conversation when the waitress passed by to check on their drinks. The timing was perfect. Leon with a gesture swirled his index finger over the drinks, signifying to bring another round.

"Detective Leon, *estoy alegre verte. Sé que estas extremadamente ocupado. Gracias por venir.*" ("Detective Leon, I am glad to see you. I know you are extremely busy. Thank you for meeting me.")

"*No tiene ninguna idea como es emocionado debo saber que eres feliz de verme.*" ("You have no idea how excited I am to hear that you are happy to see me.")

She smiled.

He continued, "You look like you stepped off the cover of Vanity Fair. How did the funeral go?"

"Oh that!"

"You have my sympathy."

"Thanks for your kind words. More than I can say about my producer."

"What happened?"

The waitress was setting the second drinks on their table. Leon nodded a "thank you." She smiled and walked away.

"She phoned me, asking, why I wasn't in the office after the funeral."

"A bit insensitive on her part."

"What I wanted to tell her was to go fuck herself, you selfish media maggot. Instead I told her, in my most dramatic and disheartened delivery that this morning I had buried my close friend and mourned for his loss. And that I didn't want to face my viewing audience with a fake smile. Whether she understood or not, I needed sometime for myself."

"I take it she gave it to you."

"Here I am."

Leon made a toast, "To you."

She smiled, "To us."

They clicked glasses.

"Didn't want to distract you from your cop duties."

"Very considerate of you."

She smiled and between sips, slowly with a melodious voice, said, "Leeoooon. Grerrrr...the lion." She looked straight in his eye with a mischievous look.

～

Juan Tequila continued his talk while the group was passing the weed around Maricela's kitchen table. "We've got to take out Paulo and a couple of his lieutenants."

"What do you mean? We?" Asked Diego.

"You guys got no choice. I'm gonna need your help or I'm fucked"

A mirror with a pile of cocaine was placed on the table by Maricela.

"Let me take a hit," said Pico.

"We'll need this shit in order to do what you're asking," said Diego.

"There'll be plenty of it once Maricela and I take control of the business... pay our taxes to the Kaliffa."

"What's in it for us?" protested Diego.

"You know that I meant every one of us... We're family," said Juan, also looking at Maricela.

"One big *familia*," she said, understanding Juan Tequila's predicament.

"But, you're fucking talking about the Kaliffa Cartel," Diego shouted, concerned about his life.

All were silent.

"Wow! This shit is tight, like snorting a snow flake, man," Tequila said with a burst of excited energy and dilated pupils.

Each one waited impatiently for his turn to snort.

~

Over their third drink, Vanessa said, "You seem to be a gentle and caring man."

"I'd like to think so."

"But, you shoot with intent to kill."

"Only unscrupulous evil-doers when shooting at me, I…"

Vanessa interrupted, "Word in the street has it… you're known for being a hard-ass cop?"

"I take on a different demeanor with villains."

"No nonsense with you?"

"Stay out of my way… no trouble… and no need to be concerned."

"And if I don't?"

"Rest assured, I will find you."

"Uhhh. Should I be scared?"

"You know the rules."

"You'll shoot me?"

"Crime and mayhem are my specialty. Let me put it another way, I hate those who hurt others."

"Not every second and every minute of the day?"

"24/7"

"And if I misbehave? You'll cuff me?"

"I enjoy precious moments like these."

Smiling, she said, "Leon, I am touched."

They looked into each other's eyes and awkwardly gulped their drinks.

"I need some strong coffee." Said Vanessa.

"I'll get the waitress."

"No, let's go somewhere else. I need some fresh air."

OLIVER SIMS

13

Urth Caffé downtown Los Angeles was crowded with people from all walks of life, enjoying Italy's finest espresso coffees. Others having selected tasteful deli sandwiches and still others were munching on scrumptious pastries.

A beautiful elegantly dressed woman in her seventies sat in the garden patio enjoying the view. She wore a two strand pearl neckless. Designer Gucci sunglasses were worn on the top of her head, like a tiara. She sipped the last drop of her cappuccino. Upon finishing, she took the napkin and gently patted each corner of her mouth.

The waiter attentive to her every need, caught her attention, as she gave a signal for her check. They conversed in Italian and shared a brief laugh together prior to her paying the bill.

She thanked the young man and encouraged him to continue his education on international studies and European art. She took her light-aqua bluish-green shawl, which was folded on the empty chair, wrapped it over her shoulder then walked to the couple siting three tables away.

"Excuse me for interrupting, I couldn't stop admiring how lovely you two look."

"How sweet of you, thank you," with a beaming smile replied Vanessa.

"Very kind of you," added Leon.

"I have learned at this stage in my life, to say what needs to be said, one may not get a second chance."

Vanessa held eye contact with the lady, then replied, "I just was telling him, life is too short to be taken for granted."

"I can see the fondness between you two. Coming from someone like me, who was married for fifty years... enjoy each precious moment like this one, with one another..." She hesitated for a moment suppressing her emotions, then continued, "One just never knows when unexpected things may occur in life."

"That is a gorgeous silk-wrap you're wearing," added Vanessa.

She gave a nod and a gentle smile. "My Niccoló gave me... just a few days before his unexpected passing."

"We are sorry for your loss," said Vanessa as Leon nodded in sympathy.

"Please sit with us for a few minutes," Vanessa suggested.

"No. I must be going. Perhaps next time."

The lady bid them goodbyes and walked to a white Audi Sedan. Her chauffer was ready to drive her away.

Vanessa took Leon's hand and gently kissed it. "See even a total stranger confirmed we're good for each other."

Leon perked up his ear upon hearing his cell ring.

"I know! You gotta go," said Vanessa.

As Leon was leaving, he leaned across the table and gently brushed a kiss on her lips.

Vanessa sighed heavily.

"We'll talk later."

"Be safe."

After Leon paid the cashier, he passed by a brown skinned, well dress dapper man with a physique, which seemed to have been noticed by both sexes.

In a euphoric state by that brief kiss with Vanessa, Leon realized, even though, this man was a total stranger to him, there was something, which disturbed him in some way... something, almost sinister about him. Leon turned back to look at the attractive gentleman, he said to himself, 'Ah, it's probably nothing.'

Temoc instead, was just about to pass by Vanessa's table. He took a step back, "Do I know you?"

"I don't think so." Answered Vanessa.

"You look very familiar... I could swear..."

After a few seconds, she announced, "I am a newscaster."

Temoc walked away, then backtracked and sat at Vanessa's table, thinking, 'God I love this country.'

~

A week later, standing outside La Providencia Restaurant located several miles north of Mexico City, Temoc lit a cigar. Reveling in the delightful aroma, he took a puff savoring the flavor before blowing the smoke out. This was one of his rituals in getting rid of buildup tension, the other, to enjoy the sexual pleasure released only by taking it from a beautiful woman.

He watched as the thin blue line from the smoke evaporated into the sky.

With his finger, Temoc signaled to the driver, who was waiting patiently with the car parked under the shade that he was going inside.

Temoc walked to the side of the restaurant where the outdoor patio was located and at the bar, he requested a shot of Trago Tequila.

Temoc instructed, "No lime, no salt."

"Always drinking the usual shit. You're consistent," said the distinguished deep voice of Hector Guerrera.

"What in the…?" Temoc, excited to see him, didn't finish his sentence.

They embraced, patting each other on the back.

"*Salud!*" Temoc with a swooping motion, threw back the tequila.

"Let's sit at that corner," stated Hector.

The gratifying taste of the Trago made its way down, soothing Temoc's wind pipe, giving a smooth sensation.

The bartender seeing Temoc preparing to pay, said, "It's on the house, as usual." He nodded to Hector.

Temoc left a generous tip nonetheless.

Hector signaled to the bartender, "Send the bottle over." Then looking at Temoc, "Let's sit at that corner table."

"How did you know I would be here?"

"Temoc, never forget I know everything," said Hector with a devious smile.

"It must be important."

"Can't I come see my prize protégé?"

"Of, course."

Sitting at the isolated corner, they drank their tequilas.

Temoc re-lit his cigar, giving Hector a serious look. "*Papa*, I know you didn't come here to talk about women or expensive horses?"

"Let's drink and discuss life."

"Discuss life or business?"

Hector patted Temoc on his shoulder. "It's all the same." Hector lit a cigarette, then continued, "My Archangel is always on point, nothing gets passed you either."

"So it is business."

"Are you ready to move product again?"

Temoc looked directly into his boss' eyes. "With the only exception that we have already discussed, otherwise we're ready."

"When will that be?"

"I'm testing the strength of the operation now."

"Get it ready, I'm sending the Belushi through the pipeline."

"How much weight?"

"160."

"Evenly distributed?"

"Majority of it… White Girl, the balance Snow."

"When?"

"Our heroin is ready, waiting for our Colombian friends to fulfil their agreement and make their delivery. When it arrives, the shipments will be every ninety days."

Temoc smiled, "Good, plenty of time."

"Excellent!"

Hector filled the shot glasses. They clicked a toast. "Here's to life, sexy women, horses…"

"And good business." Added Temoc.

"I have my own affair to attend to. Now go spend time with your woman and that new baby of yours." Instructed Hector.

~

"*Vamos*," instructed Temoc to the driver.

Sitting in the back-seat relaxed and comfortable, Temoc took in the scenery of the arid desert and plump cactus plants.

He began to daydream: '*Being tested in high school. Receiving an above average score, on an IQ test. I was always bored with my teachers and the subjects they taught. Reading and love for books that's what I have always enjoyed. Getting high with my homeboys was the greatest of pleasure. "I shouldn't have dropped out in the eleventh grade." I always had an athletic body… unique handsome face. Instead of making a name for myself playing sports and participating in the drama department. I was known for charming the girls with my ill-gotten monies. Providing drugs.*
What no one knew, I was scooping out, small time drugs dealers in the neighborhood, robbing them of their contraband goods and money. I would never be like my father. Always working hard but only eking out a living, just like the rest of my entire family had done

for years. He tried to instill in me to do an honest day's work. I was seeking out bigger dreams for myself. He was also on my case about the boys I hung around with. He made it known that he didn't care for them at all. He would always say, "Your friends are bad seeds and one day they will land themselves and you in jail. You're too smart to hang around with gangsters still in breeches."'

~

At San Quentin, Temoc had quickly realized the huge leap this prison was from the county jail in which he previously had been detained. Small home burglaries and grocery store robberies paled to the armed robbery with the intent, if need be, to commit murder and this would get him big jail time.

On his 20th birthday he got his first five year sentence in a major correctional institution. Within a short time he had come to accept his circumstances as part of the hazards of criminal life.

He made a pact with himself to do whatever it took to complete his sentence with the least amount of turmoil from his inmates or correctional officers.

Temoc became a mainline inmate at the San Quentin "Big Q" and given a prison job as a porter on the Maximum Security Unit, home to the most infamous gangster groups of the "Mexican," "Aryan Brotherhood" and "Black Guerrilla Family."

They were all seasoned gangsters, murders and hard core criminals. Temoc would always remember that very first time of uneasiness; surrounded by them and being in their presence.

As a porter his duty was to deliver meals and when needed, worked in the laundry room, cleaning, sweeping and mopping the floors. With such tasks, he had some leeway to go back and forth between jail tiers.

This was the way Cuauhtémoc "Temoc" Gutierrez would carry himself; with attitude, stature and physical built. This is what made him stand out amongst other inmates. But most importantly, it was how he'd maneuver himself by showing no fear whatsoever from the lethal men in the penitentiary. He had a distinctive elegant swagger. But nonetheless, was even more vicious then they were.

In a matter of a few weeks, in prison, Temoc started conducting business errands for the Mexican members. As a runner, he began transporting drugs and messages between their gang leaders.

However, his free hours were mostly spent voraciously reading books. His Spanish and English were above the rest of the inmates. He began entertaining his cellmates by quoting Shakespeare, reciting scripture and spewing movie and TV lines.

Stabbings and killings would take place within the prison walls but Temoc became the go-to-guy, to smuggle in shanks, which at times were embedded in his rectum so the Mexicans could complete their revenge killings.

While in prison, he thought about meeting the top man: Hector Gonzalo Guerrera. He admired Hector for being a self-made Mafioso doing time in California's renowned prison. Rumor had it that Hector was soon going to be deported to Mexico but before this would take place, Temoc wanted to meet him.

Temoc didn't know it at the time but Hector would become his mentor.

One day, Temoc heard a conversation between Hector and another inmate talking about a pending murder of a fellow gang leader.

Hector had received word that Louis "Chilly" Vegas didn't like how Hector was doing business and voiced also his dissent about his politics. This rival gang leader had questioned Hector's authority and leadership. Hector had to show moxie and force to his subordinates.

During one of his rounds, while distributing meals, Temoc approached Hector.

"I understand you need a matter resolved."

"A matter? What matter?"

"I can handle it for you."

Hector laughed, "You got balls coming up to me like this."

"I got more than that."

"You speak tough. I'm not impressed."

"I heard someone is questioning your position."

"What else…"

"He's got to be eliminated."

"Go read a book, kid."

Temoc's blood boiled but he thought best not to show his anger at the insult. "I can handle it."

"I trust no one, kid."

"I can do it."

"You got to take an oath of *omertà*."

Temoc raised his right hand.

Hector laughed, "It takes more than raising a hand."

"I'm there for you."

"And you'll never betray me?"

"Yes. I'll swear on my family."

"If you fail, you'll regret this day." Hector pointed his index finger at Temoc's face, "Failure is not a word in my dictionary. *Comprende?*"

"Loud and clear."

Hector looked at Temoc straight in the eyes studying him sagaciously. He realized at that very instant, Temoc had the making of a killer.

~

Two days later, Milo approached Temoc, who was preparing to make the lunch delivery rounds.

In a whispered voice Milo said, "The hit is today, when Chilly is in the court yard, you'll only have a couple of seconds. Hit the main arteries, drop the shank and walk away."

Louis "Chilly" Vegas standing at 6'5" and 280 lbs. was playing handball with an inmate in the courtyard. His adversary was part of the murder set-up. Prior to the hit, his job was to get Chilly playing hard in order to get his heart and blood pumping at maximum levels, making it so that he would bleed-out after the stabbing.

When Chilly's back was turned, Temoc walked up behind him and stabbed him multiple times in his neck puncturing the aorta. Blood spouted-out like a broken water faucet. As Chilly attempted to stop the bleeding with his hands, Temoc stabbed him two more times in the chest and abdomen.

Temoc dropped the shank as instructed and walked away. Another inmate, as he passed by Temoc, picked up the discarded weapon.

A rifle shot rang out setting off a general alarm.

Inmates dropped to the ground.

When the dust settled, Louis "Chilly" Vegas lay dying in a pool of blood.

~

The kamikaze-style killer was never apprehended but the criminal world gave credit to Temoc. He was revered. There were those who wanted to be associated with him at any cost.

Temoc never revealed to Hector that he was scared shit but once he got started, the fear dissipated with every blow he inflicted into Vegas' large body.

Hector's reaction was a devious smile and a nod of approval, he no longer doubted Temoc. He remembered that specific day when Temoc had said to him, "I'm here for you."

While inside San Quentin, Temoc did two more additional hits for Hector. He had become his personal executioner.

The kingpin... Hector's... for him alone, this assured his new found hitman that a job was waiting for him once his time in "Q" was completed.

Hector's deportation was eminent. Freedom was in sight. He was glad he was returning to his motherland. He knew, once in Mexico, he would be able pay off judges, attorneys and whoever else needed their pockets lined.

Temoc's tenure in Mexico was awarding and profitable. His hard work and devoted loyalty led him to become second in command reporting only to Hector.

Don Hector Guerrera would always be "*el jefe*."

It would be wise of Temoc never to slip or forget that fact.

14

Leon and Vanessa met at *"LA Live,"* the new downtown Los Angeles entertainment and night spot. The 5,600,000 square feet of ballrooms, restaurants, bars, concert and movie theaters were developed from the reparation and renovation undertaken by city hall to create the look and feel of New York City's nightlife. The once dark and seedy downtown was now vibrant palpitating with galvanized energy. The majestic skyline and bright neon lights added romance to the atmosphere as Leon and Vanessa casually strolled through the crowded street.

Leon was quieter than usual.

Vanessa took a deep sigh. "Have you ever been married?"

"Where did that come from?"

"It must be the full moon."

"Twice."

"Oh?"

"Didn't work out."

This time it was Vanessa who kept silent.

"Work - We just grew apart," continued Leon.

"I think I can understand. And kids?"

"None." Leon had his own set of questions but only added, "A true reporter... inquisitive woman."

"It's in my DNA."

Leon stopped, turned to her, and said, "OK, Miss DNA."

"Where do we go from here?"

"See what I mean."

"I'm enjoying this time together."

"Same here."

Vanessa gave another deep sigh. In a soft voice suggested, "Your place for an after dinner drink?"

"Trust me, you wouldn't want to see it." Leon laughed.

She chuckled. "Mine then."

"I'll follow you... I'll make sure not to lose you."

She smiled and cuddled close to him. "I like the sound of that."

Vanessa and Leon were waiting curbside for their cars. The valet-attendant pulled up curbside in a 2015 Porsche Panamera 4s, egg-shell white perfectly matching the beige leather interior.

The attendant exited and handed her the keys. "She's as perfect as when you gave her to me."

"Thanks for taking good care of my baby," said Vanessa.

Leon didn't say a word, as he handed a tip to the young man.

Vanessa smiled, cuddled closer to him, extremely pleased at Leon's gesture.

Leon grinned.

A moment later another valet-driver drove up with Leon's classic refurbished mint-condition metallic-grey 1979 Corvette Stingray. The masculine black leather interior gave extra beauty to the vintage vehicle.

"Nice *Popi*!" commented Vanessa.

"You like?"

"Sweet!"

They drove off.

Leon followed Vanessa down Figueroa Street, then crossed to Seventh Street, finally making their way west on Olympic Boulevard.

Leon looked in his rearview mirror and noticed a car, seemingly as if following.

His cop instincts kicked in but within a second dismissed it.

Vanessa turned left at the corner. Leon did the same. The car behind Leon also turned left.

Now, once again, Leon's detective instincts went on "alert" but stayed the course, making sure not to lose Vanessa.

She turned right.

Leon before making the turn looked in the rear view mirror once again for the suspicious car but the auto drove straight through.

Leon thought, 'Damn, I'm always questioning things.'

He made the turn and found himself in one of the higher-rent districts of LA.

Vanessa's house was located in the affluent community of Cheviot Hills, mostly single family homes.

Hers was small and modest compared to the palatial manors of her neighbors. Yet the circular driveway surrounded by a beautiful manicured landscaped front yard made it look just as grand.

This Westside of Los Angeles was known for being the residence for many actors, TV personalities and studio executives. Many of the living quarters had been and still were used for movies and TV projects because of its convenient location between the Fox and Sony Pictures studios.

Before leaving *LA Live*, she had instructed Leon to drive up all the way to the end of the driveway toward the garage, park there, then go meet her at the front entrance.

The whole night and especially now, as she was unlocking the front door, they shared a mutual anxious smile. An unseen electrical charge seemed to have been building up between them.

She locked the door behind them.

In the inside entrance hallway, Leon stood behind her, he gently kissed the side and back of her neck.

She slowly moved her head encouraging him to continue. She closed her eyes for a few seconds.

Turning her around to face him, he looked into her eyes and realized for the first time how beautiful they really were, the hazel green color made them seem as if they were two jewels staring back.

Their lips softly touched, they kissed with passion. They found themselves breathless.

Taking his hand, she led him to the living room.

"Pour yourself a drink," she pointed to the liquor bottles on the wine-stand. She continued, "I'll slip into something more comfortable."

As she was about to walk away, he pulled her into his arms and kissed her deeply.

Startled and with a pounding heart, she caught her breath.

A heavy knock was heard at the front door.

"What the...?" she looked at Leon for an answer, then went to the door.

"Who is it?"

The desperate pounding continued.

"Open up, it's me."

"Kurt?"

"Open up, damn it." He demanded.

She opened. "What the hell are you doing here?"

In a threatening voice, Kurt demanded, "Who you shacking up with this time?"

Vanessa mad as hell, shouted back, "Drunk again. You'll never change."

Leon standing behind Vanessa, asked. "Who's this guy?"

"She's my wife." Kurt answered in a slurred voice,

Leon frowned at Vanessa.

Vanessa understood Leon's questioning expression.

"We're legally separated." She turned to Kurt, "And finalizing our divorce."

"And this is my house, you bitch." Kurt then turned and pointed a menacing finger in Leon's face, "And you get the fuck out of here before I kick your ass."

"That's never gonna happen," said Leon as he stepped outside.

"Oh yeah," responded Kurt as he took a wild swing at Leon.

Leon landed a blow to Kurt's midsection. Bent over and in pain, Kurt vomited on the porch.

OLIVER SIMS

"Stop it," said Vanessa distressed by their behavior.

Leon leaned over gently putting his hand on Kurt's shoulder and in a calm voice, said, "The party's over."

Kurt attempted to speak but couldn't.

"Either you leave quietly or I'll run your ass in."

"Leon please," Vanessa said in a caring voice.

"He's been following us in a black Audi since we left LA Live."

Kurt confused, looked at Vanessa.

Looking at him in disgust, she said, "He's a cop you fucking moron."

"No!! He's the moron thinking that you're loyal."

Kurt heaving up once again looked completely lost.

"Are you stalking her?" Leon, looked at Vanessa, "What's this loyalty stuff?"

"Leon, can we just let him go. He's drunk."

"Drunk! Where's that physically built guy you walked out with at Urth Caffé?" Kurt blurted out.

Puzzled and with a more inquisitive look than before, Leon frowned at Vanessa.

"You can't drive." Leon said to Kurt, then looking at Vanessa, instructed, "Call him a taxi."

"Leon please. Let's just get him home, please." Pleaded Vanessa.

Turning again to Kurt, "Stay away from her, get my drift?"

Kurt nodded, yes.

~

The next day McCooly arrived at the office and found Leon already at his desk in deep thought. Leon felt as if he was dealing once again with deceit and betrayal; it seemed history was repeating itself: '*My stepfather Manuel was abusive to me and Mami. One day shortly after their marriage, Manuel took a belt strap to her, beating her repeatedly because she had overcooked his eggs.*

That bastard Manuel had made a previous exception but this second time; she needed to be taught a lesson. When I intervened attempting to protect my mother, Manuel took a fist to me.

I couldn't understand why my mother married such an evil man. I had never gotten over the loss of my own papa and now this villainous person was in our lives.

I confronted my mother one evening and asked, "Why did you marry him. Did you love him?"

I remember her telling me, "I married not out of love, but to protect you and your sister. A mother will sell her soul to the devil if it means to protect her children."'

"How did things go last night?" Asked McCooly. Seeing that Leon didn't respond, he continued, "How was it with Mona Lisa?"

"It's Vanessa."

"Did you tap it or not?"

"I was in full throttle until out of nowhere, her husband arrived."

"What!? Did you know she was married?"

"No clue."

Laughing, "You didn't shoot him did you?"

"No but I sure wanted to."

"Damn! Bro'."

Leon irritated, said, "What can I say!?"

"When you finally give yourself permission to get some punanny you got to deal with drama."

"Yeah, well, shit happens."

"Let's get some breakfast and fill me in."

But McCooly knew that Leon would never reveal anything, especially when it had to do with a woman.

"I instead, got together with those two. Man, the three of us…"

"The same ones as last time?" Interrupted Leon.

"Yeah! Hot and heavy."

McCooly would always fill-in Leon on every detail and he did during the breakfast they were having.

~

In Maricela's apartment, on one wall, hung a large poster of Diego Rivera's *Nude with Calla Lilies*. On the opposite wall was a tattered poster of Frida Kahlo's self-portrait.

At a corner of the room, on a table, burned a candle in a small red glass container. Above it stood a statue of the Virgin Mary holding baby Jesus.

Pacing in the apartment were Pico, Diego and Bulldog. On edge, they constantly checked their weapons and indulged often on some crystal white powder. The coke gave them a sense of superior strength and power.

Weed provided a calming and mellowing effect on Juan Tequila, who was trying to take the edge off on his uneasiness, which was running throughout all his being.

Beer quenched their thirst reducing that dry sensation they were feeling in their throats.

Juan Tequila quietly and slowly sipped his beer and for the third time impatiently looked at his watch.

1:14AM, only six minutes had passed.

Like a cancerous disease, the waiting was eating him alive.

Maricela was the only one who noticed Juan's right hand tremble as he placed his beer bottle on the table's surface. She walked across the room in an attempt to be by him.

She picked up the Glock 9 semiautomatic, which was next to Juan Tequila's beer bottle. "It's the one from Temoc?"

Juan felt the coldness of the steel as she placed it in his hand.

"Smooth isn't she?"

"Be careful, Maricela."

Seductively she said, "Hold it firm as if you were holding me."

She took his other hand and along with hers, stroked the gun gently.

"I feel the strength *Papi*, with you, we'll have the power to change our lives."

He looked at her, smitten.

She continued, "It takes balls to do this."

He held the gun firmly. "I'll think of you when I do this."

The cell rang and he quickly reached for it as if he were expecting the call.

He paced the floor listening intently.

"OK," was the only word spoken by Tequila. With his right hand and index finger outstretched in the air, he drew circles and gave the order everyone was waiting for.

"*Vámonos!*"

Juan Tequila looked at Maricela then in the direction of Virgin Mary and baby Jesus, as if seeking a supreme blessing.

No blessing came.

He made the sign of the cross nonetheless.

~

Outside an upscale collision auto body shop in Riverside, California, Juan Tequila, Pico Rivera, Diego and Bulldog were sitting inside their car, patiently staking out the place.

The shop was a front for a long time Armenian drug supplier who had ties to the Russian mob.

Juan, through Diego had found out that a drug transaction was to take place here. He looked at his watch, 3:40AM.

Tequila was given a mandate not to personally interfere with the Armenian but Temoc wanted at all costs the precious cargo. And when the time would come to deal with the Armenian, the Cartel would take care of him.

The Mafia owned geographical territories for doing business and any narcotics sold on the streets in Cartel boundaries had to pay a portion of their profits to it.

Further inside the same body shop, hidden behind a camouflaged wall, Paulo shouted to the more than a dozen young girls, who were working feverishly at their stations. "Come on people... I want this shit, cut, bagged and ready for delivery in two hours."

The *chicas* bare breasted and wearing only thongs were painstakingly cutting the coke with the right mix of boric acid and baking powder.

A gunman stood overseeing the one young girl, not older than nineteen, weighing and packaging individual kilo bags of coke then wrapping it in plastic wrap.

Still another was preparing smaller quarter bags.

In the handling of the merchandise the guards got to enjoy sampling the product. One of the fringe benefits for employing cheap labor was bartering sex for drugs.

Pico and Diego quietly took down the two watch-guards stationed at the entrance door to the collision auto shop.

Juan Tequila and Bulldog brought a battering ram from the pickup. Like a swat commander, Tequila held his index finger in mid-air and silently counted "1, 2, 3."

Pico, Bulldog and Diego with one powerful hit of the ram broke the door wide open.

With their faces covered in stockings, Tequila and his men burst in with weapons drawn.

"Put your guns down. Everyone down on the floor or die." Shouted Tequila.

Spontaneously one of Paulo's men shot his gun, barely missing Pico.

Tequila quickly shot back two rounds. The man fell to the floor. Dead.

The girls screamed hysterically and scattered in circles. Several stood frozen, others ran around looking for some piece of garment to cover their unclothed bodies.

"No one move," shouted Pico at the top of his voice.

"We are Mafia," shouted Tequila.

"Everyone's got to pay their taxes," yelled Diego.

"Bitches get your ass on the floor and shut the fuck up." Shouted Pico.

Paulo, the whole time, kept scrutinizing Tequila up and down, trying to identify the thwarted facial features created by the nylon stocking.

"Get your ass on the floor, Now!" yelled Juan Tequila at Paulo.

"Tequila!?" Paulo blurted out as he knelt on the floor.

"You know me?"

Tequila pulled his balaclava-style stocking off.

"You little nickel dime bag bitch. Do you know who I am?" Asked Paulo.

"I know who you were."

Tequila pulled the trigger.

The sound exploded powerfully as the bullet exited the gun's barrel. The force of the slug penetrated Paulo's upper chest, knocking him backwards to the floor.

Tequila had shot him at point blank.

Paulo for an instant grasped for air, his vision blurred. He could barely see Tequila standing, towering over him. Blood gushed from Paulo's mouth, he could scarcely say the words, "Fuck you."

"You should have paid your taxes homie." Tequila pumped three additional bullets into him.

15

Maricela and Juan Tequila were still in bed.

She was nestled up like a purring cat next to him. She kissed him on his chest.

"*Papi* you did good last night," she said as she got out of bed.

He pulled her back down again.

She found herself sitting by his chest.

"You bring out my manliness."

"I wasn't talking about that."

Tequila looked at her, not understanding. "The score last night, I lost count how many times we did it. I just love making love to you."

"I meant getting rid of Paulo."

"Oh that."

"Besides we didn't make love we…"

"What do you call it?"

"Plain and simple sex."

"I was so horny for you."

"And I for you… so we did it."

She got up and headed for the kitchen.

He was a few steps behind her and in no time he wrapped his arms around her waist. "You're so hot, baby."

"Don't call me that. I hate that word." She loosened herself from his embrace. "Dark Cuban coffee?"

He attempted to cuddle and kiss her once again but she avoided his advance and gently pushed him away.

Looking at his own arousal, he said, "Let's not let it go to waste."

"You want toast?"

"With jam."

"Cover that thing up."

"Call it what you want, it was real good to you last night."

"Like I said, you did good. Temoc will be off our asses."

"*Gringo's* call it a takeover hostile."

"You mean a hostile takeover."

He threw his hands in the air, "Whatever you call it. All I know is, we got drugs, money and more territory."

"You're the new boss in these streets."

"*Soy el jefe*! I'm the real shit now."

She lit a cigarette, took a drag, "We have a long ways to go."

He went to answer his cell, which he had left in the bedroom.

"*Hola* Tequila?"

At first not recognizing the voice, he answered, "Who's this?"

"You and Maricela have something for me?"

He waved nervously with his arm, getting Maricela's attention. He pointed to the cell.

She walked over and with her ear close to the cellphone, she heard, "Bring it to me." She immediately recognized Temoc's unmistakable voice.

"Where and when?" asked Juan.

"You know the place, at 8:00PM. I'm always excited when I get gifts."

"*Si, Si,* OK." Juan pressed the "Off" button.

"How much shit?"

Tequila understood precisely what she meant. Nervously he started rubbing his hands as he walked up and down the room.

"Don't know - fifty, sixty percent?" looking for Maricela's approval.

She lit another cigarette, blowing the toxic fumes high into the air. She thought for a second. "Stop pacing, you're getting on my nerves."

"What you think?"

"Give the guys their cut but our share we gotta give to Temoc. The cocaine, money, jewelry, everything."

"Are you fucking crazy?" roared Juan Tequila.

"I want to live and see another day."

"I ain't giving him a thing."

"Oh yes we are. The whole mess."

"Damn *Chica!*"

"Let *him* give us whatever he wants."

Juan Tequila unexpectedly screamed at the top of his lungs, "Fuck!" He sat down.

Maricela stood behind Tequila's chair, combing his hair with her fingers.

~

Juan Tequila carried a briefcase in his left hand, making sure the right hand would remain free, just in case he had to reach for his gun, which was tucked in his left side waistband. He was praying under his breath that he wouldn't have to go for it.

Temoc and two of his most trusted bodyguards were waiting for them at the warehouse.

Standing guard by the entrance but unseen was a third person holding a rifle.

As soon as Maricela and Tequila walked in, the guard while still holding his weapon straightaway pull- ed the heavy thick chain lowering the steel door to the ground, locking everyone inside.

Juan Tequila reached for his gun and immediately holding it by the barrel, gave it to the guard.

Maricela carried a purse, which hung over her right shoulder.

Temoc was sitting comfortably behind an empty wooden underground cable-wiring cylinder used as a table.

"Looks like you won big at the casino." Temoc said, as they approached him.

He gave Maricela a flirtatious smile, then said, "*Ho-la Chica.*"

She smiled. "It's all about you *Papi.*" She kissed Temoc on his cheek.

The men shook hands.

Temoc gave Tequila a peculiar look.

"How did you ever pull it off with a handshake like that?"

Juan Tequila glanced at Maricela.

"You took care of it that's what matters." Said Maricela.

Juan placed the briefcase on top of the massive empty wooden cylinder.

Tequila opened the case revealing three individually wrapped plastic bags with the white powder. To its side, a wad of cash was double strapped with rubber bands.

"A little over two kilos of coke and $16,706.00 in cash," said Juan proudly.

"And this," said Maricela as she emptied the purse, dumping the confiscated jewelry on the cylinder top.

Temoc smiled. Thinking, he rubbed his chin, then said, "You did good, real good."

Juan Tequila and Maricela took a small sigh of relief.

"I suggest you get rid of the jewelry," said Temoc.

"Why?" Said Maricela, surprised.

"Never wear jewelry of someone you've laid to rest. It comes back to haunt you," said Temoc.

Juan Tequila and Maricela looked at Temoc in disbelief.

"This cocaine is yours as a bonus." Then as he tossed the bundle of money to one of the body guards, Temoc continued, "Do whatever you want, sell it, snort it, give it away, I don't' give a fuck. But my product, that's a different story. You go through me and only me. How much can you handle weekly?"

"What's my cost?" Asked Tequila.

"Ten grand per kilo, it's pure, clean and white as fresh fallen snow."

Juan worked the numbers quickly in his head, '$10,000 x 3 keys equals $30,000 a week...'

He looked at Maricela seeking her support. She nodded her head ever so slightly, in approval.

Juan, turned to Temoc, "At three keys per week at the end of the month I've got to come up with $120,000."

"Bingo!"

"I can do three keys at $8,000 per key."

Temoc snickered, "There are no negotiations here. The street value in LA is fifteen to twenty thousand per key."

"Yeah, but…"

"You get uncut shit; you can stomp on it once, twice. You make a minimum five grand per key. Do the math."

"I make sixty grand by the end of the month?"

In six months you'll have well over three hundred thousand dollars – cash money in your pocket."

Juan looked at Temoc with a questionable expression. Thinking to himself, 'I can make close to a million bucks by the end of the year?'

Silence.

That moment seemed to go on forever.

Maricela broke the silence, "Hell yeah! We're in!"

"You have balls like a bull," said Temoc with a congratulatory chuckle.

Temoc's demeanor turned stern as he pointed his index finger at Tequila, "Don't fuck up, there are no excuses."

Juan Tequila looked at Maricela with a hint of venom in his blood. He turned to Temoc, with a convincing voice, "I'm in, all the way."

Temoc was not so convinced.

16

A few hours after the predawn shooting, the morning sun barely made its presence over the city as birds started their chirping.

The birds' twitters were annoying to Officer Yolanda Martinez who was already on the scene in that very early hour.

People beginning to start their hectic day didn't hear the songbirds sing. They were distracted by the city's increasing noises.

Leon arrived at the crime scene frustrated that he had to start the morning examining murder victims.

"Another bad day in the neighborhood," greeted Officer Martinez.

Leon put his latex gloves on and examined the front door. "An urgency to get in, they just forced their way."

"Leon," shouted McCooly from inside the house.

"Hey man what's the word?" greeted Leon.

"Two dead vics to start our day."

McCooly inspecting the dead body in front of him, said, "Our boy Paulo DeSilva had a rough night."

Leon, as he stared at Paulo's pale blue face, asked Yolanda, "Did you know this creep?"

"I picked him up for assault and battery, domestic abuse and possession. Everything but the drug charges got dropped. He spent time in and out of county jail."

"Those four slugs in his mid-section says something."

"What?" asked Yolanda.

"He pissed somebody off." All three laughed at Leon's quip.

"Word on the street has it that Paulo was attempting to make his bones trying to expand his territory," said Officer Martinez.

"It seems, someone with more ambition stopped him," added Leon.

"Or someone is on the defense," McCooly responded.

"Could it be part of the house cleaning we heard about?" asked Officer Martinez.

"It's our job to find out," said Leon. He covered the dead man's body. "Let's ask around and see if anyone heard or saw anything."

"We can do that detective but the majority of these residents are illegal immigrant from South America. They won't speak to us, out of fear from immigration."

Officer Yolanda Martinez waited for Leon to finish writing his notes just outside the crime scene. She watched the coroner's aides wheeling three bodies on stretchers and placed them inside the coroner's van.

"Detective Sicardo may I have a word, please?" asked Yolanda.

"What of?"

They slowly walked toward the end of the block leaving McCooly behind.

"I want to take the detective test and discuss my qualifications and get your thoughts, if possible?"

"For you, anytime, when?"

"This evening after our shift?"

"Sure... No problem. I'm thinking Eddie Cole's Tavern on 26th and Pico. My good friend Eddie used to own it. Most of all it's renowned for having a pleasant vibe, mouthwatering deli sandwiches and succulent steaks."

"Let's say 7:00?"

"Cool! See you then."

Leon answered his insistent cell as he was walking toward his car. For a brief moment he hesitated as if not wanting to take the call.

"Hey Vanessa."

"Can you talk a sec?"

"Not a good time. I'm knee deep in shit," said Leon, trying to end the conversation.

"Everything went fine... We won't have any problems from Kurt."

"I never thought we had."

"I got a restraining order."

"That's good Vanessa... I'll call you later."

"When?"

"I'll call you as soon as I can."

"I can make dinner."

"No, can't tonight."

"Is tomorrow better?"

"I'll let you know."
Leon was irritated at how he had ended the call.

~

Eddie Cole's was frequented by customers from the local SGI-USA Buddhist Community Center, who stopped there after their meetings. The eclectic and diverse patrons from the center would often go to eat, drink and share experiences with other lay Buddhist practitioners living in Los Angeles.

Their beer selection was international, making Eddie Cole's Tavern, one of best spots for sipping some of these worldwide brews in LA, not only for Angelino's but for visitors wanting to escape the tourist traps.

Julio upon seeing his good friend Leon, shouted out loud over the noise of the crowd, "Don Leon Sicardo my favorite cop where the hell you've been?"

They bear-hugged.

"Around and about... It's been a while."

"Finally took a long deserved vacation?"

"I began to wonder."

"They're always too short. Working the high rent district again?"

"I've missed your personally made Cuban sandwiches... and your New York cheese cake."

"Not me?... I'm hurt."

They both laughed.

"Beverly Hills can't compete with you."

"I keep it real."

"That's my Julio, the real deal."

"I'm expecting someone, can you get me a booth."

"An attractive Latina is already sitting at the rear booth, there toward your right," said Julio as he pointed Leon in the direction.

"She's been here long?"

"20 minutes."

"Shit! Get us two corn beef sandwiches with all the trimmings," as Leon headed towards the booth, he added, "And two pints of your finest?"

"It's already happening."

Leon smiled with a questioning frown.

Julio continued, "As soon as she walked in, she asked me, what was your favorite food and drink and placed the order."

"She's sharp."

"By the time you sit down your meal should be at the table."

"Don't forget the cheesecake."

"Dessert is on me."

"You're the best."

Officer Martinez was sitting facing the crowd. As soon as she saw Leon, she stepped out the booth to greet him.

Her hair, which she usually wore in a bun, waved freely to the back of her neck. She was wearing a gray cashmere sweater with a black short leather jacket and tight fitting jeans.

'Beautiful woman,' Leon thought to himself.

"Detective Leon."

"Your LAPD uniform doesn't do you justice."

She didn't answer.

"We'll keep it professional."

She smiled, "I took the liberty of ordering for us."

Almost if on cue the waitress arrived with the sandwiches and beers. She attentively served them, then asked, "Will you need anything else?"

Leon thanked her, and with that, the waitress left.

As Leon was ready to take his first bite, he said, "Yolanda, I read your file." He finally dug his teeth into the sandwich.

"And?"

"Aren't you eating?" He said with a full muffled-mouth.

Yolanda a bit nervous took a swig of beer from her glass.

Leon calmly, did the same, washing down that big bite he had taken only a minute before. He took another bite, this time with even more gusto. He started moaning with delight.

"And?" asked Yolanda anxiously.

"Yeah, good, real good?"

"Leon, please."

"Oh yes, very, very impressive indeed," said Leon, as he looked attentively at the remaining corn beef.

Yolanda understood that Leon was in a playing mood. She finally took a bite from her own sandwich.

"Ok. Here goes... question: 'Why did you become a law enforcement officer?'"

"I was referred by some friends who were in the Southwest Division."

"Honestly, Yolanda."

"The money was decent, so, I thought I give it a try."

"Not to save lives or catch bad people?"

"I was a gym-rat working out every day and needed a job. Becoming a police officer..."

"Would pay the bills." Interrupted Leon.

"But now it's different."

"How so?"

"I'm really enjoying working with you guys. And the satisfaction of getting those assholes off the streets."

"What was cadet training like?"

"Dramatic!"

"Go on."

"The staff was pushing me hard, you know... being a woman. But what they didn't realize... my strongest attribute was my ability to endure the physical toughness they dished out. The guys were trying to hit on me until they found out that I liked attractive women more than they did."

"I like your sincerity."

"When the word got out about my sexual preference, the gay girls were pushing on me as well. It was hell."

"Really!?" Leon sipped his beer listening to her attentively. "Didn't you have any allies?"

"While going through training?" asked Yolanda, not quite understanding his question.

"No one to lean on?"

"I did meet some people both male and female who knew what was going on and befriended me."

"I detect a 'but'..."

"But I felt the racism and sexism..."

"I bet, the Chimera raised its head a few times by simply being both a Latina and a woman?"

"Unfortunately it's still a good old boys' network. Let's be real, on top of it all, I'm of Mexican heritage."

"And so?"

"Being Latinos continues to have its battles." Said Yolanda.

"Yes it does."

"Did you have to deal with shit going through the academy?"

"Not only... You just said it. I'm from Colombia so my Mexican brethren and whites, treated me with haughty contempt."

"Do you mind sharing?"

"Another day another time."

"Of course."

"What's the hardest part of the job for you?"

"When I hear – 'officer down.' My heart drops."

Leon finished his last bite and downed the beer. "And the scariest moment?"

"Having to shoot someone with the intent to put him down. Let's not talk about it."

"It's still with me."

"Does it ever leaves us?"

"I still can't forget that first time... A silent alarm was triggered during a home invasion. When my partner and I arrived on the scene, I went to check the side of the house. The intruder was exiting a side gate. He didn't see me as he was closing it. When he turned around to walk toward the street, I shouted, 'Police... Freeze!'"

"It seems as if they always move."

"I shouted... don't move a muscle. He stopped in his tracks but I could tell he was thinking about going for his gun tucked in his waist pants. The whole time my focus was on his hands."

"That's exactly what I tell to rookie officers."

"'Don't even think about it,' I kept repeating to him. 'You as much as breathe too hard, it will be your last breath.' The look in his eyes were so intense, I could tell he was concentrating hard on what his options were."

"Thank God most of the times it's a stare down."

"But one never knows what goes on through their heads." Said Leon.

"You never know."

"Then my partner arrived gun drawn and neutralized the scene."

"Could you have done it?"

"I've learned never to assume. Always watch the hands of the suspect... Hands kill."

"Never assume… "

"Assumptions get you killed. He was smart to listen and backed down."

"Yeah, but you were smarter." Officer Martinez, chuckled.

"You don't carry the standard issued Glock but instead have a Berretta 9mm. How come?" Asked Leon.

"The Berretta has always been my favorite choice revolver."

"Why is that?"

"It's heavy, sturdy, fits well in my hand, I can shoot the wings off a fly."

"You don't say." Leon smiled.

"I was the top in my class."

"Your marksmanship speaks for itself. Where did you learn to shoot?"

"My dad. He'd take me and my brothers hunting."

"I bet you would out shoot them all."

"You bet. Living in Texas one learned to handle weapons. I went through all the channels and received authorization to carry it."

"I'm sure."

"Mr. Berretta is my best friend."

"Take care of him.

"Don't worry, I will."

"My advice is to go through the procedures for gaining your detective shield. You're in good standing as a P3 training officer. Really buckle down and know your tactical manuals and procedures. It's an extremely difficult test."

"I'm not concerned about the test. It's the brass and how they will judge me."

"You'll have some battles. Nothing's happening regarding new promotions but go through due diligence and apply for the promotion anyway."

"Yeah, yeah, but I'm lesbian, Leon. That's my big concern with brass."

"It won't be easy for you. Just show them what you're made of."

"Do you have my back?"

"You know I will. 100%. As far as I am concerned you met one of my two personal requirements."

"What's that?"

"You speak English and with an accent?"

Her laughter was contagious, "I won't let you down."

Leon nodded with approval and shook her hand as if closing a pact between conspiring partners.

Yolanda looked at a sexy lady a few feet down the corridor who was walking towards the exit.

"What is it?" Asked Leon.

Yolanda didn't answer.

At the very last minute Leon caught sight of the lady walking out of Eddie Cole's. 'Is that Vanessa?' Leon thought.

Vanessa had gone to Eddie Cole's to meet the muscular handsome stranger whom she had exchanged a few words with at Urth Caffé weeks ago.

Vanessa had stormed out after having waited for almost an hour, the stranger had stood her up. And now, she was doubly disappointed, once she saw Leon having dinner with a gorgeous Latina.

OLIVER SIMS

17

McCooly strode into the office.

Leon greeted, "My main man Cooly, what's the good word?"

"It's a beautiful day in the neighborhood."

Leon pushed his chair away from his work station and picked up a file from his desk.

McCooly walked over. "What's up player?"

Leon opened the file and started flipping through the pages. "I've got new intelligence on the Mitchell case."

"Like what?"

"It seems our boy Terry Mitchell has property valued in the millions."

"You're kidding!?"

"He owns property in Culver City, Big Bear, San Diego, Montana and Las Vegas."

"Damn!"

"The Mitchell's have a time share in San Diego at Sunset Villa, a 5-bedrooms, 5-baths, pool and beach front property. He rents out, valued at $2,900 a night. They own a luxury cabin in Big Bear, property value $950,000.

"No way?"

"That's not all."

"You're on a roll. Give it to me."

"They own a place at the Red Rock Country Club in Las Vegas, Nevada. A pretty little piece with 4-bedrooms, 5-baths and 3-car garage, valued at $1.2 million dollars."

"How did you dig all this up?"

"Good detective work, partner."

"Bull shit you got the info from the Fraud Unit."

"And with a little help from my friend at the Sheriff's department."

"Who's the 'strawberry buyer' for them?"

"Old man Sanchez… and his sweet little innocent wife Marta."

"They're both purchasing property?"

"I smell drug money."

"No doubt, let's call them in."

~

Even though the motel was located in a low-income and gang-infest community of South Central Los Angeles, Mr. Abby Patel took great pride on how he ran and maintained the family business.

The street was pitch-black again, the bulb on the lamppost shattered by a brick, had lasted only two weeks. The last time, three month had passed before the city had replaced it.

He looked out his office window but the blackness made it difficult to see what was happening all the way out into the street. As owner and manager of the Travel Lodge West, on more than several occasions, he would not ever admit to it, especially to the police that at times is was stressful dealing with his type of patrons. Rowdy habitués who on a daily basis "would have one too many or were high on who knows what."

'Most likely it would take just as long this time,' thought Mr. Patel.

His nerves were on edge and the outside darkness was being felt in his inner bones.

'Something is not right tonight,' this thought kept resurfacing in his mind.

From the rear parking lot, he heard shouting and swearing. It became louder and more vulgar. He walked to the side window and peeked through the veneer blinds.

Mr. Patel's hair on his arms stood on end. He had seen these four young men before. This time they squared-off pointing threatening fingers and hurling verbal assaults at one another. Two Latinos in their late twenties stood aggressively face to face in front of two African-Americans, whom he thought, might not even be in their late teens.

He knew these punks would always bring trouble.

Mr. Patel standing behind the blinds reached for his cell to make the call, He stopped dialing as soon as he noticed his friend Dan White drive into the parking lot. He routinely surveyed and checked on the property for the Patel's. In all the years they knew each other, Dan had become a member of the Patel family.

Mr. White lived in the area and on every possible occasion he'd come by for a chat with Abby.

Dressed in casual jeans, tennis shoes and sweat shirt, no one could tell that Dan White was an off-duty Los Angeles police officer. He stepped out of his car and started walking over to the four men whose conversation meanwhile had gotten excessively heated. He suddenly stopped. He recognized one of the punks. Immediately Dan reached for his gun strapped to his right side.

Two shots rang out.

The bullets ripped through Dan White's chest. He fell on his knees, slumped to his left side then fell on the freshly asphalted parking lot.

Patel jumped back as if he had been the one who had gotten shot. Everything happened at the speed of a bullet: quick, merciless. And yet at the same time, to Patel, it looked as if it all happened in slow motion at seeing Officer White fall down lifeless.

Traumatized. Scared. He talked to himself, "My God! Is that real?" Shaking, he fumbled at the buttons on the phone. Trembling, he couldn't get himself to push the three numbers. After several frustrating attempts...

"911, what's your emergency?"

The piercing riveting sounds of the shots fired, still reverberated in his mind.

A voice filled his ear coming from a faraway distance. Suffused. Incomprehensible to him, he finally responded, "They shot him."

A female operator on the other end, "Sir, please stay calm."

"He's on the ground..."

"Sir, calm down and tell me where you are located?"

"The Mexican man shot him."

"Sir, the location. Where are you?"

"Travel Lodge... West... Hirsch Street... 2301..."

As if the voice was echoing in a dark tunnel, he heard the dispatcher immediately put out the emergency call.

Patel's world had changed in a fraction of a second.

"That's the way, stay calm. What is your name?"

"Dan. Come quickly."

"Dan... Dan, what?"

"My name is Abby, Abby Patel."

"Mr. Patel, calmly... tell me what happened? Who was shot?"

"My friend... in the parking lot... Officer Dan White was shot."

"We're on our way."

"Please hurry, come quickly!"

Tears rolled down Patel's face.

~

9:40AM.

A husky menacing looking Latino in his early forties with tattoos covering the top of his head, hands, arms and neck, said, "No sign of him, *jefe.*"

Temoc checked his watch for the second time, while sipping his Italian-roast from Urth Caffé. He smacked his lips, "They make the best damn coffee."

He reached for his cell on the table and tapped the redial button to Maricela's phone.

"*Buenos días, Poppi.*"

"*Chica*, where in the hell are you and that little prick boyfriend of yours?"

"He's not my boyfriend," answered Maricela with a nervous undertone in her voice.

"Hope not, he's a loser."

"We'll be there in less than five minutes."

Temoc's voice became cold. "When I say nine thirty, I don't mean nine forty or ten o'clock, I mean nine-fucking-thirty."

He hung up before Maricela could get in another word.

〜

Out of breath, Maricela and Juan Tequila rushed into the warehouse; they were being escorted by the bald menacing tattooed henchman.

Temoc was sitting in his usual chair twirling a bullet from a 9mm Luger on the top of the empty wooden underground-cable cylinder.

No one dared to say a word.

The only sounds came from the spinning of the bullet and a rat noisily searching for food in an unlit corner of the warehouse.

Temoc patiently waited.

Maricela and Tequila arrived visibly shaken and stood motionless in front of him.

Temoc stopped the twirling bullet by slamming his hand on it. Maricela and Tequila took a step back. Temoc looked up at them. They could only see the white of Temoc's eyes, which added to the demonic expression on his face.

Maricela opened her mouth...

"Don't say a fucking word," bellowed Temoc.

He got up and walked behind Juan Tequila, who was trying not to show his fright.

Scrutinizing him from head to toe, Temoc sniffed him twice like a dog. "I smell your fear."

Temoc turned as if walking away but instead, with all the force of Roger Federer loading up, returned a backhand sending Juan Tequila across the room.

"*Puta*, don't you ever keep me waiting. And never have a woman call me when it comes to business. Never! Understand?" His voice was deeply subterranean; sounding as if it were coming from the bowels of the devil himself. "The next time, I will dig your heart out... with chopsticks."

Looking loathsome and dejected, Juan Tequila responded in an inaudible, "*Si*."

"Tell me about this cop you iced," demanded Temoc.

"He's had a hard-on for me for a while."

"Why?"

"I got pinched by him and got off on a technicality."

"Cops don't like it when their arrests don't stick."

"I had no choice, if he busted me again that would be my third strike. I wasn't going down like that."

"Then what happened."

"Soon as he saw me, he went for his gun. It was him or me, I shot him first."

Temoc was laughing with his buddies, more as a bravado. "I created a monster, a real fucking gangster. First he knocked-off the competition then he kills a cop." He pinched Tequila's cheek, then said, "My man."

"What do we do?" Maricela asked nervously.

"Were there any witnesses?" Asked Temoc.

"One of my boys and two *máyate* making the buy."

"Your problems are mounting."

Tequila and Maricela looked at each other, knowing that Temoc was really pissed.

"My guy won't say a thing." Mumbled Tequila.

"Did I ask you to speak?" Temoc shouted in anger.

Tequila disgraced, slowly shook his head, "No."

"You have a serious deadline to keep. Your first obligation is to me." Temoc said staring steely eyed at Tequila. He glanced at everyone. "I need to think this through. I know one thing there cannot be any distribution issues." This was said more to himself than to the others. He continued, "We don't know what the cops have… if anything."

~

'How does an immigrant from Mexico, a landscape gardener purchase multiple properties valued in millions of dollars?' Leon and McCooly, traveling at high speed through the streets of Los Angeles, had the same thought in mind.

"Based on some information received from the Fraud Unit and the Sheriff's Department, Terry Mitchell would supply all the money to his father-in-law and it was Mr. Sanchez who in turn would purchase the properties. Someone was assisting Mr. Sanchez by forging the legal documents to clear title and qualified them to purchase all the properties and without any paper-trail leading back to Terry Mitchell." Leon informed McCooly.

"If Terry was the money man, where did he get the funds on his salary?" Leon asked.

"Dirty money no doubt? When you're questioning Sanchez do it in Spanish especially if he has a heavy English accent. Should there be something of interest you want me to understand, do your English-Spanish thing."

"Me speaking Spang-lish?"

"Yeah, I'll be able to figure out what you're saying with a little English thrown in."

"My man James McCooly, long as we've been riding together in these streets of East LA, you should know Spanish fluently by now; if you learned Vietnamese..."

"Learning Vietnamese was for my survival," interrupted Cooly.

"Look around, don't you think you need to learn Spanish?"

The three beep sound, which came from the radio telephone operator was intrusive.

McCooly and Leon's chatter came to a dead silence.

The dispatcher: *All units in the area of 2301 Hirsch Street. Shots fired, Officer Down at the parking lot of The Travel Lodge West. Suspects described as a male Hispanic, no further..."*

The words "Officer Down" sent chills down Leon and McCooly's spines dramatically shifting their mood and mindset.

"Damn, who could it be?" McCooly asked.

The RTO: *"All units in the vicinity of 3A57, the PR advises suspects left the scene in two vehicles. A black*

2013 Lincoln Navigator, tinted windows, left rear bumper damaged. Second vehicle a 2015 BMW, mat-blue color, tinted windows with retro California black and yellow license plates. The BMW's plate: 4, 9, 7, (P) Paul, (D) David. Suspects considered armed and dangerous!!"

McCooly picked up the radio receiver, "3A57 we are six blocks away from location, show us responding."

"3A57 Roger, respond code 3."

When they approached the scene, McCooly responded to the RTO, "3A57 show me code 6 Adam."

Leon yelled, "Fuck," as he looked at the motionless figure on the ground.

"3A57 where is the damn RA Unit at my location, code 3, I have an officer down," commanded an impassioned McCooly.

As soon as the investigation of the crime scene came to a temporary standstill, Leon and McCooly drove through the streets of South Central searching for the vehicles and answers.

"Turn right on Buckingham Way," directed McCooly as he was trying to differentiate sounds and noises coming from the streets. He specifically focused in detecting and sighting the vehicles in question.

Knowing that a comrade had fallen always became a personal matter for McCooly, enraging him, bringing back memories of Nam. Those days when he'd bring home fallen friends from a failed mission.

For Leon instead, it would always be about his own running away from FARC in Colombia... from Sophia.

Controlling their anger, which fed on a need for revenge, was always a difficult task.

DEATH IS NOT ALWAYS SILENT from THE SICARDO's FILES

McCooly yelled at Leon, "Slow down."

"Why?"

"I got a feeling they might be somewhere around here."

"Like in Nam, surprise the enemy."

"Something like that."

Leon made a sharp right-turn on Bandini Boulevard, onto Downey Road almost hitting a food-vendor on the corner.

McCooly snapped a quick look behind him, to the right, "Got 'em. I see the BMW."

"Where?"

"Turn right at the corner, go around."

Leon drove with caution.

McCooly called the operator, "3A57 we just spotted a Blue BMW, license plate 497 PRH... Paul, Robert, Henry... at the 7-11 minimart parking lot, located at the northeast corner of Bandini Boulevard and Downey Road. We can see two male occupants. Back tinted windows obstructing view, can't see total number of suspects in the vehicle. The car is parked facing the eastside wall. Requesting Assistance. Repeat, we are in an unmarked police vehicle, gray Dodge Charger."

The operator responded within a few minutes, *"The licensed plate on the 2013 BMW is registered to Kisha Johnson residing at 2343-82nd Avenue, Los Angeles."*

"70D24 Rodger," replied McCooly.

Leon drove around the corner and entered the parking lot from the side-street and maneuvered to park behind the suspects' car, blocking it.

An LAPD black-and-white arrived, immediately followed by a third patrol car.

Leon and McCooly were already positioned crouching down behind their car doors with guns drawn. The two patrolmen immediately jumped out their squad car with guns drawn. One holding his 9mm, the other wielded a 12 gage shot gun. They crouched behind their patrol car, awaiting Leon and McCooly's signal.

One young rookie seemed to be in state of confusion as what was expected of him.

McCooly screamed at the top of his voice, "Don't shoot, do not shoot!"

Leon cowered for cover by the black and white patrol car. He reached inside the vehicle and grabbed the mobile PA system and gave the command, "Driver, place your hands on the dashboard; remove the keys from the ignition with your right hand. Toss the keys out the window..."

The driver in the BMW nervously and carefully obeyed the commands.

Leon continued, "Now, both of you, place your hands outside the windows, slowly with your left hands open the doors. Push... slowly... keep your hands up in the air as you come out."

The suspects did as instructed.

"Turn around and slowly walk backward toward me."

One of them with his hands on his head, turned around to see where he was stepping.

"Your hands up in the air," shouted Leon angrily.

The same rookie took aim with intent to shoot.

"No quick or stupid movements and no one will get hurt," bellowed Leon.

The suspects slowly walked backwards as instructed.

"That's the way. Keep coming, keep coming. Stop!" ordered Leon.

As the suspects were being handcuffed, they were read their Miranda Rights.

OLIVER SIMS

18

One of their own was down.

They had two suspects who had been placed in separate holding areas but no confessions nor motives had been given.

The prison's grey concrete walls were completely bare – no pictures or photos. A small metal table was in the center of the room with two uncomfortable metal chairs on opposite end. A third chair was isolated in the corner. One side wall had a two-way mirror. From the other side of the wall, Rory could see and at the push of a button could hear any verbal exchange of the interrogation.

One of the two shooting suspects was escorted and literally tossed by McCooly into the dungeon-like room.

Hand cuffed behind his back, the suspect yelled, "Why am I here, I didn't do anything. Get these goddamn things off, they're too tight."

McCooly turned the suspect around and unlocked the cuffs, then said, "Watch your tongue."

"Hey man this is fucked up, I told you…"

"Yeah, Yeah, I know, you didn't shoot anyone. Have a seat. You want any water?"

"No. I don't want any damn water, what I want is to get the fuck out of here."

"Sit down and watch your mouth."

The stymied and agitated muscular suspect shouted in a commanding voice, "Ok, gimme some water."

McCooly's look was stern. "You can't do any better than that? You're not at home and I just saved your black ass."

"Saved my ass!? What the fuck you talking about?"

"You and your gangster friend are persons of interest in a cop killing. Do you know what that means?

"Nah… You tell me."

"When a cop draws his gun it's for one purpose only."

"And what is that?"

"To shot with the intent to kill. If the gun is in hand, our objective is to make sure you never see the light of day, ever again."

"You cops wanted me dead?"

"There are cops who want revenge. They'll shoot first, ask questions later."

"You're a cop, why didn't you shoot?"

"I'm interested in the truth."

"What you trying to say… black lives matter?"

McCooly walked over to Monroe and stood toe to toe, eye to eye, then said, "Punk all lives matter. Don't come in here talking about your 'black lives matter bull-shit.' If that were the case you and your hoodlum friends wouldn't be killing each other and innocent black people in our own neighborhoods."

Grimacing in anger and wiping sweat from his face, "Look Bos, I didn't do anything. I'm thirsty," said Monroe.

Seeing that McCooly wasn't going for the water, he changed his attitude. "Detective, can you get me some water?"

McCooly shrugged his shoulders.

~

The room where Leon was interrogating his suspect was hot and stuffy and with the ventilation system turned off, made it almost impossible to breathe.

The suspect looked at his black Movado watch. Only twelve minutes had passed but to him it seemed like hours. He felt like a caged animal. He kept saying to himself, 'They don't have anything on me. I can take their bullshit and whatever else they dish out.'

Leon reviewing a file, positioned himself comfortably in a chair in the corner of the room facing the suspect.

"My name is Detective Leon Sicardo."

Leon read from the file, "Your name is Otis Marshall, correct?"

The suspect didn't answer.

"For the record, state your name."

Rolling his eyes, "Yeah, my name is Otis Marshall."

"Mr. Marshall, do you know why you are here?"

"Something about some cop being shot."

Leon looked at the perp with grave concern. "You understand or have any questions regarding your Miranda Rights which was read to you? Anything you say can and will be used against you."

"And for the record I didn't do it."

Leon took these words as frivolous verbal rhetoric.

~

In the other room McCooly interrogated and pressured Monroe for information.

"Tell us about the shooting?"

"Bos, I told you, I don't know what you're talking about."

"Where were you tonight?"

"I was with my home-boys hanging out."

"We have creditable, reliable information that you and Otis Marshall were at the Travel Lodge West."

"Where? – Nah. Nowhere near there."

"Where were you around seven this evening?"

"At a bar."

"What bar?"

"A place called Pip's."

"Pip's! That's all the way across town on La Brea and mid-Wilshire. How is it that you were in that part of LA at the time of the shooting?" McCooly's voice became louder.

"Bad timing I guess?"

"So you don't know the time of the shooting?"

"What? Nah man I'm clueless."

McCooly slammed the file shut. "Let me tell you what we know. We know that a police interrogation is not a fair fight. We have all the experience and all the means to get information and answers. By the time we're done, you'll be crying for your mama."

"I didn't do a thing."

McCooly walked over to the side of the table, leaned over a few inches from Monroe's face and said, "You'll have wished that cop had shot you."

The suspect showed no signs of concern.

"And now - with your dumbass, we'll bust you for carrying a concealed weapon," McCooly commented in a pronounced grave voice.

Leon knocked on the door where McCooly was interrogating his suspect.

As McCooly was ready to step out, he turned back to Monroe and said, "Whether you shot Officer White or not, you're doing time."

Once outside and with the door shut, "What you got?" asked McCooly.

"My guy was there."

"He confessed?" asked McCooly surprised.

"No. It's a gut feeling."

"Can't convict him with that," said McCooly frustrated.

"They're playing tough guys."

"We're going nowhere like this. I think we should pull our joker card."

Leon said, "I'll tell my boy the sad news."

They went back to their respective interrogation rooms.

~

McCooly as soon as he stepped back into the room, said, "Your future doesn't look bright. You'll be old and gray before you see a full moon. And God forbid, don't let that gun be the murder weapon…"

The suspect sat quietly, listening, seemingly not bothered.

McCooly shook his head, "Damn! You're in trouble." He paced the room, then said, "You sit there and flex, meanwhile I was informed, your friend cracked."

Monroe looked at McCooly with suspicion, but didn't say a word.

"Your mama will be crying, 'my baby, my baby.'"

"Leave her out of this," shouted Monroe.

"Don't you get it, we know everything about your sorry ass. We know she paid your bail the last time you got in trouble."

"You don't know shit."

"You're a mommy's boy, a little bitch." McCooly persisted, "Your sisters are always covering up and taking care of you."

"That's bull-shit, I can take care of myself."

"Oh really like when your sister…" He opened the file looking for a name, then continued "…your sister Veronica vouched for you at her job. You got her almost fired from the company and she got suspended without pay, because she tried helping your flaky ass."

"Fuck you," in anger shouted Monroe.

"You're a little bitch. Once we send you away, I'm putting out the word that your name is Margo."

The suspect pushed the table knocking his chair over. He stood up and in rage went at McCooly. The detective deflected Monroe's aggression, immobilizing him with an arm grip putting him in a choke hold. Monroe was pinned to the wall.

"That was a stupid move." McCooly from behind pushed Monroe's face hard against the concrete wall, in his ear he whispered, "When you're in lockup these are some of the things they're going to do to you…"

Monroe couldn't speak due to the restriction from the forced position.

"And being the momma's boy that you are, they'll take what they want. And another thing don't call me BOS. You can call your jailers that, when you're in lock down. But I am not your - Bag of Shit."

McCooly threw Monroe in the chair, "Ask me why I became a cop?"

"I don't give a fuck why."

McCooly stared down at Monroe, like a boxer preparing for a prize fight. "Go on punk, ask me."

"Why did you become a cop?"

"I became a cop; one, out of respect for my ol' man. He was a hard working family man. Did everything by the book. He battled Jim Crowism all his life, flew planes and fought in a war to show his loyalty to this country; only to be shot down at home, because of the racist system. Then here you come, young black and stupid. You and your kind totally disrespecting the elders who fought and died to make this country a better place for black people."

"What the hell you talking about?"

"My father was robbed at gun point, pistol whipped and left for dead in a home robbery."

"What do you want from me, I didn't do it?"

"Yeah, but you contribute with the drugs and violence you push on the streets. It's all part of the black-on-black crime wave. Ask me, what's the other reason for joining the force?"

In a slumber tone, Monroe asked, "What's the other reason?"

"I hate dirty, racist police officers. You see there is something in common between bad cops and thugs."

"What's that?"

"They're both criminals."

Monroe looked down at the table.

"Look at me. Too many people of color sacrificed much - for assholes like you and few bad cops who run loose in this city."

"What? You're the enforcer?

"No, I'm just a man, one of many doing his job. But you - I'm ready to release you're ass to those insidious white men in blue."

"Man, what you talking about?"

"Those guys who possess a detainee whom they dislike, only because of your color and breed. They want revenge. If you can't help me, I can't protect you."

Silence.

"I want a deal!" muttered Monroe.

"It depends on what you have to offer."

"No. Not until you guarantee me full immunity."

"Immunity?"

"And protection."

"This better be more than good," said McCooly as he leaned in to hear what Monroe had to say.

"Otis and I had heard what happened to Paulo but we needed our supply."

"Paulo DeSilva?"

"And guess who showed up instead...? Juan Tequila."

"You, Mario and Juan worked dealings together before?"

"No we got high a couple time, shit like that, but no business. That's why we didn't think twice about buying from him. He boasted that he was put in charge and all dealings moving forward would go through him. Paulo was out and he was in."

"Do you know who killed Paulo?"

"My money is on Juan Tequila."

"What makes you say that?"

"He shows up wearing a gold crucifix with a red ruby in the center."

"So!"

"It was one of a kind, an original made in Mexico. Paulo's mother gave it to him before she died. He would never have given it to someone like Juan. Me and Otis were there when this white dude shows up. We didn't know he was a cop."

"Tell me about the killing of Officer White?"

"Juan killed him right in front of me. That white guy shows up looks at Juan... like as if he knows him. Juan says, 'Oh shit.' Takes out his gun and shoots the dude."

"Just like that?"

"Just like that."

"Where's Juan?"

"He's probably in Mexico by now. You'll never find him."

"Why do you say that?"

"Because that's where they go when the shit hits the fan."

McCooly handed a pad and pen to Monroe and instructed, "Start writing."

~

When Leon had walked back to his interrogation room, he dragged a chair and sat next to Otis Marshall.

"You're not going home anytime soon. Help yourself by telling us something we can take to the District Attorney."

Silence.

"Let's cut with the bullshit, they want your ass."

"Who are... they?"

Everyone...I need to tell you that your buddy Monroe is on his way to the infirmary."

"What!? What happened?"

"Fell down the stairs while being transported."

"That's bull-shit, you guys fucked him up."

"The wolves are at the door, your friend Monroe just sold you out."

"Now I know your lying, he'd never do that."

"You're going to do time for weapons charge, but the killing... you're looking at life."

Otis sat in the small dungeon-like room, telling himself, 'Getting popped for selling drugs is one thing, killing a cop, I'll be damned if I'll take a rap for something I didn't do.'

Overwhelmed, for the first time Otis felt fear. At twenty-nine years of age, he was coming to the realization that his life was on the line.

Leon looked at him without saying a word.

Otis whispered a few words.

"Can't hear you," said Leon.

"I want a lawyer."

OLIVER SIMS

19

With a sense of accomplishment, McCooly and Leon stood outside the precinct, taking in the fresh night air.

"Let's start tracking down this 'Tequila' guy and hope he really didn't flee to Mexico," said Leon.

"This routine is getting old."

"What?"

"This shit! Mexican crosses into our border, commits crime then returns to Mexico to escape justice. Literally never to be found again."

From his pouch, Leon took a Partagas D6 cigar, evenly cutting its end. He lit it, took a deep draw and watched the thin blue smoke escape into the heavens.

"Another needle in a haystack," commented Leon.

"The Mexican authorities won't provide any assistance. Latinos here won't provide information due to reprisal. A year later they return to LA and start up where they left off," responded McCooly.

"And the most frustrating thing, we can't go and get 'em."

McCooly looked at his watch, "I'm starving it's after ten."

"I'm buying the first round?"

"Cool."

"I'll see you at Eddie Cole's."

They got in their own cars and drove with the wind at their back.

～

Maricela Barrone lost her temper and in an uncontrollable rage, screamed at Juan Tequila's latest bravado.

"Killing a cop! How fuckin stupid can you possibly be!?

"*Mami*, I had no choice… it was either him or me."

"I can only imagine how Temoc is going to take this. And you left witnesses behind…"

Maricela's fear and anxiety welled up knowing that every cop in Los Angeles would be looking for him. She took a deep drag from the menthol cigarette, trying to calm her nerves but at that moment it had no effect. She chain-smoked, pacing up and down the room.

She continued, "Should have been you, motherfucker."

"Homie, get out of LA. Go back to Mexico," said Pico Rivera, who was listening attentively to every word.

"How do we keep the operation going?" asked Maricela.

With trembling hands, she stumped her cigarette in an ashtray she was holding, then said, "Temoc warned us... there are no excuses..."

Pico stepped forward, "Me and the other homies, we'll run things..."

"Every month the money's gotta be on time," replied Maricela lighting another cigarette.

"Even if we need to take care of the *mayates*... But for now let's get you out of here," said Pico, hurriedly.

"My *primo* will get me to Mexico. Can you really handle the shit until I can get back?" Tequila, asked concerned.

"Don't worry."

"I'll tell Temoc what happened," suggested Maricela.

"No *mami,* I will do that," said Juan with a look of distress on his face.

Maricela for the second time within the week, felt fearful and uncertain.

~

Eddie Cole's always pulsated with the rhythms of jazz, salsa and R&B.

The architectural structure of the tavern was designed with details of heavy wood and steel beams, which extended from floor to the ceiling. The distinctive look was created by the hanging paintings of attractive original artwork created by international and local artists. Mounted behind the bar was a replica of the self-portrait of Vince Van Gogh in a variety of colorful chalk and pastel oil. Van Gogh's piercing blue eyes seemed to overlook patrons sitting at the bar and nearby tables.

A classic Hammond B Organ set in a corner on the platform-stage, waiting for the next instrumentalist to bang out some melodic notes. Musicians performed their craft recreating the sounds of Miles, Monk and Jimmy Smith. Some of the younger players incorporated a little Hip Hop with R&B overtures.

For Leon and James, this was always a reprieve from the activities of crime and chaos. They were unwinding over a couple of beers.

McCooly craved for a real taste of New Orleans crawfish, gumbo and catfish, it's exactly what he ordered for himself. He suggested for Leon to do the same, and he did.

Twenty minutes later, a petite barmaid with a short haircut, rich dark-chocolate skin and almond-shaped eyes, placed the plates on the counter.

She was already familiar with Leon and Cooly, "Here's your cup of gumbo and poor-boy's special for two of LA's finest." She said.

"Cool," McCooly responded.

"*Gracias*," Thanked Leon.

They enjoyed a moment of solitude, savoring their beers and sandwiches.

McCooly looked up at the TV, "Hey man, isn't that your girl?"

Vanessa Compose was reporting the follow-up lead story of Officer Dan White's shooting.

Leon asked the bartender to crank-up the volume.

The room quieted down as the level was raised.

Vanessa's voice was heard more clearly as she reported on the latest LA gangland shooting.

—

Leon sat in his car in the parking lot of Eddie Cole's thinking whether to call her or not.

After a few rings, she answered, "Well, this is a surprise?"

"I'm pleased that my number is registered."

"Detective."

"So, I've been relegated to detective once again?"

"I thought you kicked this girl to the curb?"

"As I recall, the message was, 'I'll call you later.'"

"Leon that was two weeks ago."

"Sorry."

"You caught your quota of bad people today?"

"Where are you?"

She didn't answer.

"You up for a nightcap?"

"You call me at 11:30 at night, Leon..."

"That is, if you don't have a stalker following you?"

"And you with Latinas."

"What are you referring to?"

"I'm not referring to anything."

"What, you're developing a sense of humor now?"

"Stop it Leon."

"What's eating you?"

"Nothing."

"I thought you were the one who wanted things to be out in the open."

"Ok, then, here goes. Two weeks ago you were at Eddie Cole's. Dinner with a young Latina lady – after you had told me that you couldn't meet me."

"Oh that! – Officer Yolanda..."

"Officer my foot..."

"Now hold on! She was out of uniform..."

"Oh I'm sure. Leon, please don't lie to me."

"Vanessa, I'm not."

"I mean you swim with the sharks, carry a gun and shoot bad people. Sure you're not scared?"

"Scared of what?

"Scared of picking up a phone and making that call once in a while?"

"Whaoww! I'm getting a whipping."

"We're both creatures of the night... just getting off work."

"So what do you say?"

"Leon... Leon Sicardo, what am I going to do with you?"

"You can tell me when I get there."

Leon remembered exactly where she lived.

He left Eddie Cole's parking lot and headed east on Pico Boulevard. Over the city's speeding limit, Leon propelled his muscle-car through the dark of night just like an Indy 500 race driver. Eventually onto Venice Boulevard, he took another left onto Motor Boulevard. The blatant roar of the vintage Corvette Stingray engine could be heard from the distance of two city blocks. Finally, he reached the quaint community of Cheviot Hills in less than 15 minutes. Leon quickly turned off the ignition not wanting to wake up any of Vanessa's neighbors.

There was pep in Leon's step as he walked up toward the front porch.

He found the door unlocked. He walked in.

"Hey... It's me."

He closed and locked the door behind him.

No response.

The lights upstairs were on.

"Hello," Leon gave a shout from the bottom of the stairwell.

"Make yourself right at home. Fix yourself a drink," instructed Vanessa from upstairs.

"How about you... anything?"

"I'll have whatever you're having."

As Leon went to prepare the drinks, in the middle of the floor there was a discarded pair of dark blue Valentino Rockstud Rolling Pumps. To the side he notice, Vanessa's pinstripe blue suit tossed on a Chinese antique rosewood flower-design chair; the suit's matching skirt at its feet.

In the quietness he could hear running water filling the bathtub.

After having prepared the drinks, Leon walked slowly balancing them as he started up the stairs.

Upstairs he passed a room, which was Vanessa's home office. The bookshelf nearly covered one entire wall from floor-to-ceiling and a large desk with a computer and two thirty-inch monitors were off on the opposite side of the room. Pictures, awards and artwork were hanging on the other walls.

The room, which he had just passed, must have been her multimedia room. A large fifty-two inch television with the latest sound system was mounted on the wall and was visible from where he was standing.

He approached the wide-opened door to the masterbedroom. On its knob hung a silk light-blue blouse.

"Drinks are being served." Leon announced in a soft voice.

Silence.

He walked toward the hypnotic sound of running water.

He knocked on the opened door. He could hear the splatter and slushing of bathwater. Not receiving an answer, he asked, "Should I leave the drink... here?"

"Bring it in."

Matching red bra and panties were on the floor near the entrance to the bathroom.

Standing halfway in the doorway, Leon said, "Is that the scent of papaya?"

"It could be my candles."

He stepped in and saw her submerged covered in bath bubbles.

A few scattered lit candles were on the floor.

"Come join me." Her quick-forward response took Leon by surprise.

She saw his reaction. "Let me take a sip," pointing to the drink.

He hesitated for a second.

"You going to just stand there?"

He handed her the drink.

She took her first sip and gave the glass back to him.

"Didn't care for it?"

"Are you coming in?"

He placed the drinks on the sink counter and immediately undressed.

She stared at his naked body, "Uhhmmm."

She opened her arms and welcomed him in the warm scented water and as soon as he stepped in, she took him in a tight embrace.

Their kisses were passionate. An exhilarating rush of desire ran through their veins. It seemed as if two lost lovers had finally found one another after a very long absence.

Leon kissed her neck tasting the flavor of the soap. 'Papaya?' It didn't matter. He kissed her breasts slowly, finding himself immersed in the water kneeling, kissing her belly button.

He came up for air.

She laughed in seeing his hair stuck to his forehead just like a drenched little poodle.

After kissing, fondling and washing each other, she said, "Let's get out."

Before he could respond, Vanessa was already standing outside the tub reaching for bath-towels.

She quickly dried his hair. Disheveled. She reached and hugged him tight.

Never leaving her embrace he slowly got on his knees. Still holding her by the waist he stared at her neatly trimmed pubic hair.

"Beautiful, absolutely beautiful." Leon's only words.

"You like?"

"Had no idea you're a natural redhead."

She laughed.

"My daddy is Mexican but grandmother was a red-bone from New Orleans."

He buried his face at the center of her core.

"Leon! Please... do..."

Vanessa moaned in delight.

～

The exquisite aroma of fine toasted coffee made its way to the bedroom. The fragrance lingered forcing

Leon to wake up and open his eyes. The large bedroom curtains were closed but Leon could see the walls painted in a light beige and egg-shell white trim.

The white fluffy comforter made the bed look larger than a king size. In the corner on the tan leather love-seat was his jacket and pants neatly doubled over.

He didn't remember having folded them. Even his boxer shorts had been neatly placed on top of his pants.

On the armoire were Leon's LAPD badge, car keys, cell phone, Glock 9mm and his ankle compact gun.

Leon was still in bed.

Vanessa walked into the room carrying a tray with a cup of coffee, a small spoon, a cloth napkin, a creamer and a small bowl of sugar, she greeted. "Good morning Mr. Sicardo,

"Back to formalities?"

"I can make breakfast if you like."

He took a sip of coffee, then said, "I can't but would love to take a rain check."

"Love me and leave me, the story of my life."

He got out of bed, with coffee in hand, went to the armoire, before checking the time on his cell, he took another gulp. "Oh shit,"

"Now what?"

"Look at the time: 6:42."

"So!"

"I'm meeting with my Lieutenant first thing this morning and he's a real asshole. I can't be late."

"It's not every day a girl gets a surprise booty call in the middle of the night from her favorite law enforcement officer."

"You must have a dozen guys who you can call at a drop of a dime."

She gave him a suspicious look. "It's not that kind of party Detective."

"Life's already giving me a hard time, so you don't have to."

She pointed in the direction of the bathroom, "There's a towel and wash cloth on the sink."

"Do I get a rain check on that breakfast?"

"Maybe!"

He walked over to where she was standing and gave her a deep kiss.

~

On his way to the precinct, the words kept echoing in his mind, 'You must have a dozen guys who you can call at the drop of a dime.'

His thoughts went back to his childhood days: *"There is nothing more refined than the love of a mother for her children," My mother, Darcia Abelina Sicardo, at times had said to her close friends. She was a woman with innate beauty, fine curves and with long black hair. She accented her trailing flock of hair, bouncing-off her shoulders with a colorful simple red, yellow or sometimes white ribbon.*

The humidity and brilliant sun enhanced the color of her skin giving it a constant radiant brown tan. Her beauty was envied by women and blooming young girls who wanted to be just like her.

Over a drink or a smoke, men in the cantina would often speak of their intense unrestrained sexual cravings for her. But it was my father, Eduardo Fernand Sicardo who won my mother's heart. My father was known throughout the community as a gentle, quiet,

talented artist. He wrote poetry, had a distinctive voice, played the guitar and above all was a gifted painter; capturing Mama's allure on canvas. Even though his paintings were flawless, no one in our destitute community could afford such beautiful art.
My father's purpose for living, was to enjoy an artist's life and to passionately make love to Mama. Life was meager yet joyful for the young lovers.'

When Leon was born things began to change for the worst. When Leon's sister Rocio was born, life for the Sicardo family became laboriously painful.

20

The late afternoon sun in Mexico was high.

Hector and Temoc were wearing sunglasses to protect themselves from its vibrant brightness. Sitting on the back porch, they just finished their lunch of *gorditas* with red salsa, vegetable chilies *rellenos* with walnut sauce and cheese, Mexican-style corn-on-the-cob and *carne asada*.

"*Mi amor*, lunch was delicious and now I have business to attend to."

Hector's wife knew exactly what he had meant.

"Thank you *papa*. Don't forget we have plans this evening," responded Catalina with a contagious smile. "Please, be back in a couple of hours."

Before leaving, Hector looked at his daughter with admiration, gave her a kiss and a gentle peck on her cheek. He then gave a soft kiss on his wife's lips.

Temoc, respectfully, gave Catalina and Hector's daughter his goodbyes.

Hector and Temoc left the open air patio and walked to the Dodge Ram pickup where the chauffer was already waiting.

They drove five miles on a well paved road, an extension of his property. Three heavily armed men followed closely in a black Lincoln Navigator. They barreled-down with their vehicles onto the city owned graveled-road leaving a trail of flying dirt and dust behind them.

Arriving at the destination, two men with automatic rifles posted as sentry at the entrance, recognized Hector. They immediately came to attention and waved them trough.

After another mile, they saw the large warehouse. The structure looked uninhabited.

Inside the air conditioned and well maintained building were laborers stationed on several assembly lines, methodically, carefully measuring, cooking, preparing and packing cocaine, multitasking, working like bees

One man driving a pitchfork truck, hauled slates of packaged marijuana, stacking it at the one end corner of the edifice.

On a side wall, from floor-to-ceiling, on steel framed slats were evenly stacked bundles of 1Kg cocaine packages.

Every person became even more alert and keenly aware of their responsibilities as soon as Hector and Temoc entered the huge room.

"Isn't this a beautiful sight?"

"We've traveled a long way from smuggling marijuana to being the biggest supplier of cocaine and heroin throughout California."

Temoc just nodded, *si.*

"Pure, uncut... for the simple pleasure of the stupid Americans."

Temoc nodded once again in agreement.

"Come let's go to the office."

Temoc followed him.

Don Hector Gonzalo Guerrera's life was surrounded by beautiful and lavish artifacts. His warehouse office, however, resembled a low level government employees' work station. It consisted of only one small window and bleach-white stucco unpainted walls. An old wooden desk looked as if it had survived a journey from Spain, back at the turn of the last century.

Hector poured two shots of tequila, "Here's to my new deal."

They both lifted their glasses.

"To the Colombian Cartel," said Temoc.

"To my renegotiated deal with those bastards?" laughed Hector.

"You're right boss," said humbly Temoc.

"I'm busting your balls, Temoc. Knowing you had my back was crucial. Give you credit by having them guaranteeing a steady supply and a reduction in price to us."

"Now we can stockpile it and finally fulfill the demands of those hard-up gringos." Said Temoc as he downed his drink.

"Take a few days off. Spend time with your women, because I'll be sending you back next weekend."

Hector filled the shot glasses once again.

~

The special mandatory meeting, which had been called for all the law enforcement officers within the LAPD, to attend, had started punctually at 8:00 AM. In the large auditorium a capacity crowd of officers anxiously awaited the arrival of Police Chief Gary Maryland, the highest ranking officeholder of the prestigious police department.

Leon and McCooly, sat anxiously waiting to be briefed before they began their shifts. McCooly leaned to his side and in a low voice asked Leon, "How did last night go with you know who?"

"Vanessa."

"I want details. Did you..."

Before Leon could answer, the command: "Attention!" was given as the Police Chief entered the room.

Everyone stood at attention.

"Officers thank you for your attendance, please be seated." In his uniform decorated with pens and medals, he looked gallant like a general assessing his troops. He perused the room with eagle eyes. The Police Chief continued, "Many of you may have already heard that the Board of Police Commissioners has adopted a new policy titled, Special Order 40."

Whispers and grumbles were heard.

"Order. The Department is sensitive to the principle that effective law enforcement depends on a high degree of cooperation between the Department and the public it serves." He then read: *"The Department also recognizes that the Constitution of the United States guarantees equal protection to all persons within its jurisdiction. In view of those principles, it is the policy of the Los Angeles Police Department that undocumented alien status in itself is not a matter for police action. It is, therefore, incumbent upon all employees of this Department to make a personal commitment for an equal enforcement of the law and service to the public, regardless of alien status."*

Officer Yolanda Martinez raised her hand and asked, "What's the purpose of the new mandate?"

"The Los Angeles community has become significantly more diverse during the past several years with substantial numbers of people from different ethnic and socioeconomic backgrounds migrating to this City. Many aliens, whether from Latin American, African, Asian or European countries are legal residents, others are undocumented and are residing in the City without legal sanction."

A white detective sitting next to his Asian-American partner who were assigned to the heavily populated Chinatown community, asked, "How are we supposed to fulfill the duties of our job, especially when we suspect the person in question may be an illegal alien?"

The Police Chief said, "Let me read further to answer your questions: *"In fulfilling our obligations, the Department will provide courteous and professional service to any person in Los Angeles, while taking positive enforcement action against all individuals who commit criminal offenses, whether they are citizens, permanent legal residents or undocumented aliens."*

Since undocumented aliens, because of their status, are often more vulnerable to victimization, crime prevention assistance will be offered to help them in safeguarding their property and to lessen their potential in becoming crime victims. We need this measure to enhance community and police cooperation."

A Sargent asked, "So what you're saying is: police service will be readily available to all persons, includ ing the undocumented aliens."

"That is affirmative. We want to ensure a safe and tranquil environment. Participation and involvement of the undocumented alien community in police activities will increase the Department's ability to protect and to serve the entire community."

Another officer asked, "Chief won't this order hinder our efforts in getting crime related information from Mexicans and Asians who might be here illegally?"

"On the contrary, the mandate was passed in an effort to encourage undocumented residents to provide information and report crimes without intimidation from LAPD."

"What's ICE's position on this procedure?" asked McCooly.

"Immigration and Customs Enforcement will continue identifying, investigating and dismantling vulnerabilities regarding the nation's borders and infrastructures. They will focus on immigration issues. We will focus on our responsibilities to protect and serve those who live in our communities."

"When does it go into effect?" asked Leon.

"Immediately."

~

Leon sat at his desk lost in thoughts staring at his computer: *'People in the barrio said my stepfather was*

a corrupt policeman, a Sargent in the Colombia Natio-
nal Police department at the local precinct. The rumor
was that my mother was having an affair with him. A
hush-hush word spread throughout the community that
one day he had my father killed.
Twelve months after his burial, my mother and Sargent
Manuel Gezana were married. Many said that she had
married Manuel to assure for herself the safety of her
children.
Under his protection her children would not get in-
volved in any gang-violence or mayhem, which con-
stantly besieged them in their village.'

McCooly walked in, "The good doctor Princess
Liang called, she wants to meet us in her 'private
suite.'"

"Good, I need to get away from this thing." Leon
grabbed his gun and holster.

~

No words were spoken as Leon and Cooly entered a
quiet, eerie, windowless large room.

Hanging on the wall, next to electronically-con-
trolled doors, were white lab coats with faint brownish
red blood-stains. The unavoidable odor of raw-flesh
lingered amongst stainless steel tables and jars of
formaldehyde. Perfectly aligned on the wall were face-
shields resembling welder's helmets next to electric
saws and other bone-cutting equipment. The shimmer-
ing stainless steel sinks were meticulously clean.

"It's weird, it always feels dull and sticky walking
on these tile floors," said McCooly.

"I guess no matter how many times one washes and scrubs these floors, you can't remove years of caked-on dried blood."

Suspended from the ceiling were florescent lights that propelled a luminous brightness to the chamber.

"It's morbid," said Leon.

"What do you expect we're in the freakin' autopsy suite."

"Detectives," greeted Dr. Diane Liang.

"Word has it, you are looking for us." Said Leon.

"What'cha got for us Doc?" McCooly's asked.

"What I have – Is, who Got, Got."

Leon confused and not understanding, looked at McCooly, "What!?"

McCooly laughed, then said, "Doc you been hanging out too long with the brothers on the East side."

Ms. Liang born in mainland China immigrated with her family to Chicago at the age of twelve. The family moved from city to city; Boston, DC, even lived six months in the freezing cold of Buffalo, New York. Ever since moving to America she always wanted to fit in.

"What I am saying detective Leon, we have several victims who got caught being at the wrong place at the wrong time, executed with the same weapon and same modus operandi."

"Thanks for the clarification." Leon smiled.

"You guys got bodies dropping everywhere. It's difficult to keep up."

"And they all have a duplicitous story to tell." Added McCooly.

"And we're here to shed light on their dramatic narrative. As an example…" She walked to a wall nearby, pulled on a silver door handle, opening what looked like a refrigerator. She withdrew a slab holding a lifeless body. She repeated the process two more times. "Officer Dan White, Paulo DeSilva and the third vic, whom we are still attempting to identify, were all killed with a Smith & Wesson M&P 9mm."

"Are you sure?" questioned Leon.

"Science can only reveal the truth," quoted Dr. Liang.

McCooly looked at Leon, "Our suspect, Tequila has been busy."

"There's more," continued Dr. Liang.

"You have our undivided attention," said Leon.

She walked to the end of the room and pulled out another slab. "Mario Lopez here, was killed in Boyle Heights with the same gun as Terry Mitchell, his wife and daughter in Culver City."

"And what model was that?" Leon asked.

"A Glock 9mm."

"Are you sure about that?" asked McCooly."

"The science of ballistics can't lie. I confirmed with Culver City PD, the gun used there matched the one for Mario's murder."

"So we're looking for multiple killers?" asked McCooly.

She didn't answer, then confirmed, "One more thing, some of the victims killed with the Glock had the identical talon markings on the upper torso as well."

"Two different killers?" asked Leon.

"Are they related or connected in any kind of way?" Asked McCooly.

Again, she didn't answer.

"Only way to find out is to track down this Juan Tequila character," replied Leon.

"We better step on it, he's a Mexican and all roads lead to Mexico."

～

Lieutenant Rory sat on the edge of Leon's desk sipping coffee, staring at images on a large white easel board, which had photos, lines, arrows and circles connecting suspects of victims followed with question marks.

"Your report Leon is detailed. I just wish we knew where to begin, to find this Juan Tequila character. We have any idea where he is laying low?"

"No. The last known address from a previous arrest came up empty handed," answered Leon.

"The streets will reveal something." McCooly chimed.

"It always does," replied Leon.

"I don't give a rat ass where he is, find the bastard. No cop killer gets away on our watch."

～

The Dodge Charger speeding passing Venice Boulevard was traveling north on Fairfax Avenue. The computerized female metallic-voice from Map Quest instructed: *"In 350 yards turn right on 18th street."* This time Leon had traveled alone to the location. He made the turn and noticed the quietness of this middle class community in the Miracle Mile district. The voice returned: *"In 75 yards turn left on Ogden Street, your destination is on your right."*

Leon noticed in the middle of the block an LAPD patrol car. Directly across the street was a 1987 flatbed pickup truck. A Hispanic man in his fifties was leaning on a rake and talking to Officer Yolanda. As Leon approached them, Yolanda Martinez said, "Detective Sicardo, this is Mr. Esteban Cortez, the gentleman we discussed."

Leon extended his hand, "*Buenas tardes.*"

The soft spoken man with a deep raspy voice replied, "*Buenas tardes.*"

"*Señor* Cortez thank you for coming, you can speak freely to us," informed Officer Martinez.

"*Muchas gracias por tu ayuda.* We appreciate your service and we understand your status here as being an illegal," added Leon.

"Because you are helping us, Immigration and Customs Enforcement will not know of this conversation." Confirmed Officer Martinez.

At first reluctantly, Mr. Cortez spoke in English, with a thick Mexican accent. "I have been here twenty years, I make no problems."

"Where in Mexico are you from?" Asked Leon.

"I'm from Toluca. But Los Angeles is my home now. I am a professional gardener, do much work in Beverly Hills, Santa Monica, all over LA."

Officer Martinez looked at Leon and said, "We are meeting on this side of town, as to not be seen by anyone who knows him."

"I understand. What is it you want to tell us?"

He looked around, to see if anyone was watching.

"You're safe," reassured Officer Martinez.

"I am scared for my *sobrino.*"

"Why? What's wrong?" Leon asked.

He looked down at the sidewalk avoiding eye contact, trying also to avoid the question.

"What is it Mr. Cortez?"

"If they find out, I speak to you, very bad for me."

"Who's they?" asked Leon concerned.

"Kaliffa."

"Your nephew is involved with Kaliffa?"

"*Si.* He's a good boy but his *amigos*, bad, very bad."

"Who's your nephew?" asked Officer Martinez.

"Pico Rivera."

~

Walking into the third floor squad room with buoyancy in his stride, Leon greeted McCooly who was sitting, working at his computer.

"How did your deposition go?" asked Leon.

"The bad guy will stay in jail, for now."

"I've got new intel thanks to Officer Martinez."

"As I've said the streets always reveal something."

Leon walked to the large white easel board and wrote the name Pico Rivera under Juan Tequila Pasquel.

"Yolanda's source gave us this name."

"Who gave him up?"

"The kid's uncle, Esteban Cortez. The old man is trying to do the right thing."

"He must not like evil doers."

"He's trying to protect his sister's son. I might add, Mr. Cortez is an illegal from Mexico."

"Does ICE know about him?" Asked McCooly.

"Hell no! And we don't want them to know, I gave him my word we would keep Immigration Services out of this."

"What about this Pico cat?"

"Apparently he's one of Tequila's boys."

"Good let's get a hold of Pico, he can point us to this Tequila character."

"Not that simple."

"Why?" Asked McCooly.

"Word is - our killer Tequila Pasquel is hiding in Mexico."

"It's a big country. Where in Mexico?"

"They think he's headed to Tijuana."

"He could be anywhere. Ecatepec, Acapulco, Mexico City.

"Let's get with LT. and fill him in."

"Is your passport in order?" McCooly asked as he gathered his files.

They headed toward Lieutenant's office.

~

Lieutenant Rory started reviewing the notes submitted by Sicardo and McCooly, he suddenly stopped, looked at them both, "So you think the Terry Mitchel murder in Culver City and the other drug related killings in Boyle Heights are all somehow linked together?"

"Our instincts and information is pointing us in the direction of the Kaliffa Cartel," answered Leon.

"Before I send you guys tracking off to Mexico on a possible wild goose chase lets follow-up on loose details here at home. Where are we with Frank Ruiz, Terry Mitchell's supervisor?"

"We were on our way to talk to him when we got the call regarding Officer White." Answered McCooly.

"Also check in with Captain Jenkins at the LA Airport Police. See if he has anything new to contribute."

"If it's warranted, I'll begin to arrange looking into arrangements for getting you guys to Mexico."

"Come on partner we got our marching orders." McCooly signaled to Leon to get a move on.

21

The garage looked almost like any other ordinary auto body repair shop, if it were not for the more than a dozen hand guns and rifles spread out over the work benches.

A young heavy set Latino lit the torch and began cutting through a metal slab inside the trunk of a 2016 Ford Fusion. Once he finished cutting, he shut off the torch. Hidden inside the secret compartment were three freezer size baggies filled with yellow pills.

The heavyset Latino went to cut part of the right fender. Smoke and sparks flew, the flame melted away the metal as if it were butter. He pulled apart the section from the chassis of the car.

As soon as it cooled off, the welder stuck his hand inside and withdrew four duct-taped brick-shaped bundles.

Maricela literally took them out of his hands and delicately made a small incision in one of the bricks. On the point of her knife she tapped the tip of her tongue in the white flakey powder. She took a hit in each nostril. Her brain lit up like flood lights turning what seemed to be a dark cave into a brilliant glowing brightness.

"Wow!"

"Here," she handed the knife and package to Pico who did the same steps as Maricela.

"Damn this shit is fuck...ing good!"

"What are you looking at?" She asked the young welder.

"Where's my hit?" He asked.

Everyone stopped. They all stared him down. He nervously looked around, "What? What'd I say? I just asked for a hit."

"It's not for employee consumption. Unless you want to pay for it," replied Maricela.

"Let's get it cut, packaged and ready for delivery. We have a schedule to meet."

"This is too easy," said Pico.

Maricela's look was harsh, "Don't get happy. We have another car coming next week. We have a lot of work to do."

"Who put you in charge, away?" demanded Pico.

Maricela took the gun from the tool box and pulled the sleeve back, pointing it to his head. "I work for Temoc and you work for me. We clear?"

His hands shielded his face, cringing, "Don't shoot, you're in charge."

Standing in the doorway observing, Temoc clapped his hands, steady and slowly. "Damn *Chica*, I like the way you handle your shit. Next time anyone gives you a problem shoot 'em."

The welder handed Temoc the bag filled with pills.

Temoc held it as if measuring its weight then handed it to Maricela.

"Hand these out to whoever buys the heroin and cocaine."

"What is it?"

"It's Methamphetamine."

"What do I charge for it?"

"You don't. Give it away as sample to your customers."

"And when they come back asking for more that's when we charge 'em."

"*Chica* your momma didn't raised a fool." Temoc smiled delighted.

~

In his apartment in a rushed, rapid pace, Juan Tequila frantically threw clothes in a suitcase and backpack. Everything he literally owned was crammed in those two travel bags.

He took a hit off the joint hoping it would calm his nerves.

Temoc's muscleman instructed Tequila, "You don't have time for that. Get your shit and let's go."

Pico Rivera and Maricela anxiously awaited for Tequila to get going.

"You got everything?" asked Maricela.

"My world is now in both your hands."

"It's all good" said Pico.

"It's temporary," Maricela reassured Tequila.

"Just make sure you guys handle the business."

"I was going to say the same thing to you," Maricela responded.

"What did you tell your people?" Asked Pico.

"That I'm headed to the south of Mexico for work. That way my *familia* won't bother looking or ask so many questions.

Maricela looked at him, concerned, "Temoc set everything up, you're in good hands," still trying to re-assure him.

"I will."

The muscled henchman angrily gave the final word, "Would you get the fuck out of here."

~

Tequila had never seen roaming buffalo on an open prairie. He made sure to drive within the speed-limits while admiring the magnificent scenery with its lush green fields. Snow run-off from the mountains fed into the Gardiner River, which swiftly flowed directly be-hind the small country town. He could visualize the trout hopping over and between the rocks in the freez-ing water.

Two saddled horses were tied to a post outside Dave's hardwood store. If it hadn't been for the parked vehicles in front of The Stage Coach Inn and The Corral Restaurant his imagination would take him re-motely back to an old far-west setting.

Tequila pulled up to the gas pump, cut the engine off and took a deep breath. He then exiting the vehicle feeling a sigh of relief.

The sun still visible but was slowly starting to disappear behind the snow-cap mountains.

A fatigued Tequila began fueling his own gas.

A battered pickup driven by a middle aged man pulled up on the other side of the gas pump.

The man with weather-beaten-skin was bald except for a few strands of stringy long blond hair, which peeked from underneath his baseball cap. He got out of the truck and before he began pumping his own gas, waved to the person behind the window. He then asked the person on the opposite side of the pump, "Hey you speak English?"

The Latino taken by surprise, "What?"

"Do you speak English?"

Aggressive and abrasive, Tequila answered, "Yeah, I speak English, why?"

"Hey man, loosen up your *Fruit-of-the-Loom,* I... just making conversation."

"Been driving for a while... a little tired"

"Where you coming from?"

"Billings, Montana."

"Where you come before Billings?"

"You ask a lot of questions."

"We're just friendly... from these parts. Where you headed?"

"Like I've said, you ask too many damn questions."

"Hey man just trying to help, you look lost that's why I asked."

"To Gardiner, Montana."

The gringo laughed, "*Chico* your standing in Gardiner."

"This is it!?"

The man with weather-beaten-skin spat his chewing tobacco on the ground, "Yeap, Gardiner, Montana all of 3.7 miles and 875 of us. Hey is that an F-250?"

Tequila looked around confused, not understanding the question. "

"Is that an F-250 Ford pickup truck?"

"Ya, I guess?"

"They say you can carry a lot a shit in there."

"I guess..."

"What's your name?"

"Juan."

"What brings you to Gardiner?"

He answered slowly, "Looking up a friend."

"You look like a friend of ours."

"Who would that be?"

"You look like 'Tequila' Pasq... Our friend... Temoc..."

A chill went through Juan's spine.

"You're Redneck?"

"No, he's waiting for you."

"Where?"

"You'll know... Come on Pesly..."

"It's Pasquel."

"Whatever! We know every fuckin' thing. We knew when you got lost outside of Billings."

Tequila didn't say a word.

"Get on Highway 89 going east. I'll meet you a mile outside of town. You'll follow me to where you need to go."

Driving in the charcoal-black night, without having any idea as to where he was headed, Juan Tequila was apprehensive about following him. "Where the hell am

I going," he blurted out loud. 'Can I trust this fuckin' gringo?'

He struggled in following the two red tail lights forty feet in front of him. The road was bumpy and full of pot holes. They drove fifty minutes outside of town. He could only see what looked like two, then three lights in the far distance.

Not to be taken by surprise he pushed a button on the CD deck opening the panel and retrieved his hidden 9mm, placing it into his jacket's pocket.

He smelled the clean scent of pine trees and the aroma of burning wood. A moment later he saw a lodge cabin with smoke spewing from its chimney, he seemed to have found himself in the middle of nowhere.

Tequila followed the pickup to an open area in front of the cabin.

"Here we go," he said out loud to himself.

He saw the gringo walk to a makeshift wooden garage and turn on a generator switch, which powered light to the immediate area. A short stocky man held a Colt M16 automatic rifle and another taller man with a reddish-brown thick beard holding a gun pointing to the sky, stepped out of the cabin.

The rifleman walked to Tequila and shouted, "You're late."

Tequila didn't say a word.

The buffed bearded mountain-man said, "Forgive my friend he gets a little excited when strangers come around. Did you have any problems?"

"Got lost outside of Billings. You Redneck?"

"The one and only."

"You look nothing like your picture."

He smiled, "Mug shots never look right. Are you loaded down?"

"Yes."

"Park your truck in the garage and let's get down to business."

Once inside the barn, Tequila asked, "Where am I?"

"You are officially in Montana at the entrance of Yellowstone National Park.

Tequila asked Redneck, "You got the money?"

"Money? What money? Redneck turned to the other guy, "Nubs, you got any money?"

"Na, all I got are these." He lifted his rifle with one hand and grabbed his crouch with the other.

Tequila's mouth became dry and drops of perspiration began to bead on his forehead.

Silence.

Juan looked over the entire small room and thought. 'Shit three to one.'

Redneck stared at Tequila and burst out laughing, "Relax homie. We got your money."

Juan Tequila wanted to scream but all he said under his breath was, "Motherfuckers."

Redneck enjoying the intense moment, said, "Temoc and I have a good business relationship. We don't want any issues with the Cartel."

Redneck gave the gringo a nod, who quickly left for the garage.

Putting his hand on Juan's shoulder just like a friend, "It'll take a minute to dismantle the truck and get the goodies... want a drink?"

Without waiting for an answer, Redneck pulled out a bottle of whiskey and paper cups from the cabinet.

"How do you know Temoc?" Sarcastically Juan added, "What, you guys were bosom buddies or something?"

"We were appreciated by important people inside... in lockup. We were on opposing forces, he being with the Mexicans and me with the Whites."

"How did you guys start working together?"

"Temoc and I share the same mindset."

"What's that?"

"It's all about the money. People respect us for that."

Sipping his whiskey, Juan's face showed a dislike for it.

"It ain't tequila."

The short stubby gringo returned with a gym bag, gave it to Redneck, who in turn opened it. Seeing all that cash, Redneck smiled.

"Here you go one hundred thirty thousand dollars. You want to count it?"

"Yes."

While Tequila was counting the money, he asked "How did you get the name Redneck?"

"The jig-a-boo's gave it to me before we deployed to Afghanistan."

"You let them call you that?"

"Conflict has a way of bringing unlikely people together."

"Tell me about it."

"It was in the heat of battle that made me realize being surrounded by Blacks, Jews and Mexicans wasn't a bad thing especially when they have your back and we're all shooting at the same enemy. Until I went to war, you would have never seen me being civil around them or your kind."

"You mean Mexicans."

"Yep, they all became my buddies especially when the rag-heads started shooting at me."

They all laughed.

"It's good business to know some blacks and to speak a little Mexican." said Redneck.

"Spanish."

"Ha?"

"You mean... Spanish."

"Spanish, Mexican it's all the same."

The stubbly gringo gave a nod to Redneck.

"We're good Pasquel. You got your money and we have our three pounds of heroin and ten kilos of coke. Thank Temoc..."

"And the methamphetamine?" Interrupted Tequila.

"Give samples to our best clients for their customers.

"And if they like it?"

"We'll add it to our list, next run."

22

Leon was driving to LAX International Airport.

McCooly in deep thought sat in the passenger seat. "What's your read on Frank Ruiz?" Asked McCooly.

"I'm not sure yet."

"Can't put a handle on it, either."

"Yeah, a modest home with very expensive art work and sculptures."

"Are we saying that a man from Mexico who is a supervisor at LAX can't appreciate and own expensive artwork?"

"I get a little suspicious when several pieces of art that cost in the neighborhood of fifty to a hundred grand…"

"How do you want to handle Frank?" interrupted McCooly.

"Let's probe and see where it takes us."

~

Frank Ruiz was talking on the phone. As he finished the call, he waived them into his office.

"Would you like some coffee, a cola?"

"No thank you," said Leon.

McCooly declined with the nod of his head.

"What can I do for you detectives?"

"We're doing some follow-up work and we're hoping you could add anything new regarding the Mitchell's case?" Asked Leon.

"I can't get over his passing...."

"Murder," injected McCooly.

"Yes, murder. But why would anyone do such a vicious thing?"

"Something that deliberate and brutal was intended to be a message," replied Leon.

"A message!?"

"A statement, not to cross them," said McCooly.

"Who would be that demented to do such a thing?"

"Our suspicion is, Mitchel was involved with the Kaliffa Cartel."

An uneasy choking sound was heard in Frank's throat as he was slowly sipping his coffee.

"What makes you think that?" asked Frank.

"Our training and experience," answered Leon.

"That's why we're here talking to you," interjected McCooly.

"You don't think I had anything to do with any of this?"

"Did you?" Asked Leon.

"No. Of course not," replied Frank taken aback by Leon's blunt question.

"Do you recall seeing any strangers visiting Terry Mitchell prior to his death?"

Frank sat back in his chair, looked up at the ceiling. In reflection, "Hum, I do recall two guys, I've not seen before speaking to him."

"When?"

"The first time was several months ago and then again about a week prior to his..."

"You hadn't mentioned this before." Interrupted McCooly.

"Because I'm just now remembering it."

"Can you provide any details, description, what they looked like?" Asked Leon.

"Maybe East-European in their thirties."

"Why do you say European?"

"Because of their accent. Sounded more like Russian or from that area."

"Do you have any idea what they might have wanted with Terry?"

"All I know is they looked threating, scary."

McCooly immediately asked, "Why do you say that?"

"One pointed and poked his finger in Terry's chest. Both guys were physically built. Like they had been working-out in some kind of prison yard."

"What do you know about prison yards?" asked McCooly.

Frank smirked nervously, "Only what I've seen on TV." Then quickly added, "Maybe it had something to do with his lady friend."

"What lady friend? In our first conversation you told us Terry was the loyal faithful husband and father.

Now you're telling us something different." McCooly said annoyed.

"He was loyal. He mentioned that a couple of times he had gone out with someone... just a friend. That's all I know."

"Is there anything else you forgot to mention to us?" Asked Leon.

Frank ran his fingers through his hair. "Positive."

"You think of anything, no matter how small, you give us a call." Concluded McCooly.

～

Staring out the open window, Juan Tequila could smell the fragrance of the Grand fir and White Bark pine trees surrounding the skimpy Yellowstone Lodge and Motel where he was staying.

Wild flowers growing in the lush green fields along the side of the mountain was a pleasant reprieve for Tequila. However, he wasn't sure if it was a blessing or curse being in Montana.

It was the perfect hiding place but he missed the street life, the hustle and fracas created together with his home-boys in Los Angeles. What he missed most was the flirting, foreplay and uninhibited sex with Maricela.

If given some time, he would prove himself to her in that she would eventually be his woman. But for now, he'd have to contend with the peace and solitude of Billings. He gulped down the last drop of beer and without a second thought threw the bottle out the window.

"Fuck it! I need some excitement." He said out loud and walked out the door of his bunker.

His cell rang.

"Hello."

"How's my Mexican doing in the land of cow-boys?"

"Maricela, baby, I'm going *loco*, waiting for your call."

"I got good news and bad news."

"Baby, I missed you."

"Don't give me this 'baby' shit."

A pause of hesitation, then he said, "Gimme the good news."

"You get to come home. The bad news is you have unfinished business to attend too."

"Like what?"

"Don't play stupid, you know exactly what I mean?"

Silence.

Juan Tequila rolled his eyes up to the celling.

More silence.

"No more than four days." Said Maricela.

The call dropped.

Tequila turned his phone off. Pissed off as hell, he said with a trembling voice, "Shit!"

~

A stocky young Mexican, in his twenties, handling the baggage on the tarmac at American Airline was sweating excessively under the hot and humid skies of Mexico City. He took his red, white and blue bandana off his head and wiped the perspiration off his face and the back of his neck.

His uniform was soaking wet as he loaded luggage, baby strollers and boxes into the cargo-bay of the 737 jet liner.

The ground crew, flight attendants and pilots were preparing for the departure of flight AA0212, from the busy Mexico City International Airport.

The baggage handler carefully placed a matching pair of large beige-and-brown Louis Vuitton suitcase off the tarmac, onto the plane's cargo wide rolling belt.

He placed several softer luggage around the Vuitton suitcases as if to protect them from getting damaged.

He gave thumbs up to the attendant who was standing in the doorway, signaling that everything was ready "to go." The handler got in his vehicle and drove off.

Twenty-two minutes later the plane took-off on time, bound for Los Angeles.

⁓

At LAX the ground crews were busy making preparation for the arrival of American Airlines flight AA0212, from Mexico City to taxi into its assigned gate.

The engines shut down.

The cabin door was opened from the outside, passengers departed the plane.

On the tarmac, two baggage handlers hurried unloading the cargo. The Louis Vuitton suitcases were picked up immediately and put on the right side of the transport baggage truck.

The driver drove to the terminal bay to unload the cargo. The Vuitton luggage were given a special marking and put on the conveyor belt for delivery to the baggage claim area.

A young Latino smoking a cigarette, waited outside, leaning on a black Cadillac Navigator. He became nervous as an airport patrolman walked in his direction but was relieved when he was told to just move his vehicle.

He did as instructed and drove off.

Inside at carousel number 3, an elegant dressed Latina retrieved the Louis Vuitton bags and walked outside. Composed and unfazed she stood curbside as she looked in both directions for her driver. Not seeing the car after a long 15 minute wait, she began to perspire. She pretended to be talking on her cell as two patrolmen passed by in their squad car. She checked her watch for the second time. Less than four minutes had passed.

'Where the fuck is he?' She thought.

She sighed with relief when she saw the young driver flash his lights. He approached and stopped the car with a slight screeching of the wheels, jumped out and opened the door of the SUV. He hurriedly assisted the passenger and her bags into the car.

Once the driver got into the diving lane, Maricela speaking in perfect Spanish, told him, "Let's go. Pay attention to the road and avoid mistakes."

"*Si*," the driver merged onto the traffic exiting the airport.

23

The homes on the 1200 block of Ridgeley Drive, in Los Angeles, were impeccably well-manicured.

His posture tall, erect and wearing dark sun glasses, he seemed to be more like an FBI agent than an LAPD Detective. McCooly looked in the direction of the street. On-lookers in luxury automobiles and Latino nannies pushing infants in strollers, looked at him with curiosity.

Leon observed the neighborhood.

Standing on the front porch of the two story house, he noticed that the lawn was evenly cut and greener than the others. Well-tended flowers were in front and along the sides of the house. A red 2016 Matador Lexus 350 was parked in the driveway next to a shining white Chevy Silverado pickup-truck of the same year. *Sanchez Landscaping Architectural Design Service* was displayed and advertised on its side doors.

Leon rang the bell to the house.

Within few minutes, standing in the doorway, a man wearing cowboy boots, Levi jeans and with a large silver-gold belt buckle, speaking with a heavy Mexican accent, said, "*Hola*. What is it?"

"*Hola*, Mr. Sanchez?"

"*Si*."

Raymundo Sanchez looked older than his fifty-five years due to his weather-beaten face; working the fields in the colder climate of winter to the blistering heat of summer.

"I'm Detective Leon Sicardo and this is Detective James McCooly of the Los Angeles Police Department. You remember, we called earlier to speak to you and your wife Marta, regarding the Mitchell family."

"*Si*, Yes. Come in."

They entered the conventional yet well-furnished house.

Leon thought, 'They're Catholic, the Madonna shrine in the corner, multiple crucifixes of Jesus on the wall. Old palm leaves left over from a long time ago Palm Sunday. There are artifacts from Mexico, a few clay pottery and sculptures with mounted paintings and pictures on the wall.'

"We appreciate you taking time out of your day to speak to us," said McCooly.

"Are you a Galaxy fan?" asked Leon.

Raymundo a little surprised by the question, "*Si*, I like soccer."

Leon pointed to a corner, "I noticed the LA Galaxy ice chest and seat cushions."

"I, Marta…we take the grandkids to see football but today they come get the tickets and go with their friends."

Marta entered the room at that very moment. Petite, fashionably dressed, her haircut short and black seemed as if she had just come back from the beauty salon. Raymundo introduced her to McCooly and Sicardo. After a polite handshake, they all sat down in the living room.

Speaking in Spanish, Leon asked Raymundo if he preferred to speak in English.

"No problem, English is OK."

"You have a lovely home Marta. May I call you Marta?" Asked Leon.

"*Si*, detective that is OK."

"There's nothing like owning your own home." Added McCooly.

"Where are you from in Mexico?" asked Leon.

"Guadalajara."

"That's a lovely city. I'm from Colombia."

"How long have you lived in Los Angeles?" Asked McCooly.

"I live here soon nineteen years."

"Your English is good." Added McCooly

"*Gracias*, I mean, thank you."

"Tell us about Terry and Lucinda," asked Leon.

"I… *Dios, Dios*. I miss them so much," mournfully answered Marta. Tears rolled down her cheeks.

"We are sorry for your loss… that's why we are here. Correct me if I am wrong, Lucinda was your adopted daughter?" Asked Leon.

"She was our niece. When her parents were deported is when we adopted her," replied Raymundo.

"When was that?" Asked McCooly.

Attempting to control her emotions, Marta replied, "She was eleven."

There was a moment of silence.

"They were a loving family. Terry would give you anything you asked for." Said Raymundo breaking the silence.

"How so?" asked McCooly.

"He gives plenty to his church, much money to the children's schools, friends and family that need help, Terry was always there."

"He helped Raymundo set up his own business," replied Marta.

"Is that so?" McCooly asked.

"Business was not so good, Terry gave me money to help buy equipment and hire men to work. He told many, many friends about my work. Now we do good."

"How many people work for you now Mr. Sanchez," asked McCooly.

"I have twenty-two peoples. Two to four peoples on each crew depending on the job and two or three peoples in the office."

"What about Terry's friends?" asked McCooly.

"He doesn't have many friends."

Leon got up, walked across the room and picked up a framed photo on top of the cabinet. "May I?"

Raymundo nodded his approval.

Leon looking at the photo, "Is this man, one of his friends?"

Marta answered, "That's Francisco."

Leon showed the photo to Cooly.

"Tell us about Francisco," inquired Leon.

"That's Francisco, me and Terry on a fishing trip," explained Raymundo.

"Where was the fishing trip?" Asked McCooly.

"Puerto Vallarta, Mexico."

"Nice boat!" Commented Leon.

"*The Lucinda.*' Terry named her after his wife?" Said Marta.

"That looks like a 40 footer." Said Leon.

Boasting with pride, Raymundo said, "Much bigger, it's 60 footer and sleeps ten peoples."

"How long did he have the boat?" Asked McCooly.

"Almost two year."

"Have Terry and Francisco been friends for a long time?" Asked Leon.

"They took many trips together, Vera Cruz, Playa De Carmen… mostly Mexico."

"Mr. and Mrs. Sanchez, you've been very helpful. Can you think of why anyone would want to hurt them?" Concluded McCooly.

"No, they good peoples." Answered Mr. Sanchez.

"I'm sure they were. McCooly do you have any other question?" Asked Leon.

McCooly pointed to a different framed photo on the stand, "Who's the attractive lady in that photo?"

"That's Francisco's daughter." Answered Mr. Sanchez.

"This is Melon, a daughter from his first marriage." Concluded Marta.

"Anything else?" Asked Leon.

"No, I'm good," replied McCooly.

Leon handed them his card. "If you think of anything please call us."

Driving back to the precinct, McCooly said, "Leon, when I pulled the financials on Terry Mitchel, no boat was referenced, let alone one sixty feet long. And there's no record of money going to *Sanchez Landscaping* either."

"That's because and this is the kicker, when I checked on Lucinda's employment at Scenic Drive Financial, it's a store front."

"That was what my gut feeling was telling me," said McCooly.

"That's what you call, a nice adopted daughter." Commented Leon.

"Leon, here's another kicker, Terry's supervisor, Francisco a/k/a Frank Ruiz lied to us."

"Let's call him into the station and see what else he lied to us about," said Leon.

"Consider it done."

Leon staring at Cooly, asked, "You got that look, what's up?"

"There is something about that photo."

"What is it?"

"I can't put my finger on it but there's something."

~

Smoking a cigar, Temoc and three members of his crew were anxiously waiting for the black Cadillac SUV to enter the auto repair shop.

Driver and passenger exited the vehicle. The driver immediately went to the back of the SUV and unloaded the suitcases consigning them to one of Temoc's workers.

The elegantly dressed Maricela, wearing a Gucci cropped blazer on a cream-colored tight fitting skirt, greeted Temoc with a bear hug.

Temoc said in Spanish, "Glad to see you *Chica*, any trouble?"

"No problem, smooth as silk." She said, as she glided her hand over her own silk blouse.

"How did it feel carrying forty pounds of pure uncut cocaine and a million dollar practically in the palm of your hands?"

"Fucking exhilarating, exciting as hell."

They laughed.

"Just think you get to do it again before you have time to buy a new Chanel bag. Let's have a drink. The rest of you guys get to work," ordered Temoc.

Temoc and Maricela walked into his small office where he took a tequila bottle and poured some in two shot glasses. He handed one to Maricela.

"All our distribution lines are one hundred percent operational," informed, Temoc.

"Ah, Partida Tequila Elegante, such refined taste, Temoc," said Maricela, as she smacked her lips trying to savor every drop.

"To the victors, the rewards. *Salud.*"

"*Salud!*"

~

The loud whirling sirens and flashing lights of the ambulance were turned off as two paramedics rushed out and with a gurney hurried into the County Jail building. Standing in the doorway was a County Sheriff officer who led them through a maze of several hall-ways and corridors.

In the very last room, a police officer was vigil over an African-American male motionless on the ground, completely drenched in blood.

"Shit," said the head paramedic. He knew by the amount of blood on the floor this man most likely had bled to death.

"How long ago was he shanked?" He asked.

The County Sheriff officer didn't know what to say and looked at the vigil officer for an answer.

"He was already down when we got to him," replied the officer.

"From the looks of things, maybe twenty minutes," responded the frantic assistant paramedic, who was using both hands applying pressure on the victim's punctured neck wound.

She immediately started to administer CPR.

"Let's get him on the gurney and out of here," instructed the head paramedic.

In a stream of yellow, red flashing lights and blaring sirens, the ambulance sped through the streets, transporting Otis Marshall's lifeless body to the closest emergency room.

24

Francisco Ruiz sat comfortably yet isolated, surrounded only by the four grey naked walls of the interrogation room at Sicardo and McCooly's precinct.

McCooly and Leon entered the concrete silo, as Francisco yawned expressing his boredom and lack of concern.

"Frank, we didn't mean to keep you waiting," said McCooly.

"My time is valuable why are you wasting it?" Responded Francisco.

"Is it Frank or Francisco?" Asked Leon.

"Detective Sicardo, what's so important that I had to come to the station? It's Francisco."

"We have a few things we'd like to clear up," said McCooly.

"I've answered all your questions."

"We are fact-checking tightening up loose ends."

"Like what, may I ask?"

"Let's start with your relationship with Terry Mitchell?" said McCooly.

"What relationship? I told you he was a subordinate, a good worker. What else can I tell you?"

"It has come to our understanding, he was more than an employee," responded Leon.

"Well, your information is incorrect."

"What kind of fishing do you like to do?" asked McCooly.

Francisco's expression was vague and with a tinge of confusion, "What fishing?"

"You know, fishing, do you prefer fresh water or deep sea?" Asked McCooly.

"I'm not a fisherman."

"You see that's why your ass is in here. You don't respect what we do?" Agitated, McCooly responded.

Francisco's voice turned angrier, "I have no idea what the hell you're talking about."

"We're talking about you lying to us. We have creditable information you were good friends with Terry and his family." Said Leon.

"You're *loco*." Without thinking, blurted Francisco.

"You've been on many overnight fishing trips throughout Mexico with Terry."

Silence.

Leon broke the stillness. "The fact is, Terry was more than an employee under your supervision at the airport."

"Let's talk cars," said McCooly.

Francisco irritated, looked steely in Leon's direction.

"What kind of car do you drive?" asked McCooly.

"What's with the games fellas?"

"I assure you this is no game. What kind of car do you own?" repeated McCooly.

"It's a Mercedes-Benz. Why?"

"Model?" asked McCooly.

"An S450." Answered Francisco.

"That's your everyday day car?" interjected Leon.

"Yes."

McCooly continued questioning, "What does your wife drive?"

"A Lexus."

"Which model?" Asked Leon.

"I don't recall."

"Let me help you. Your wife drives a Lexus LS 460, runs about seventy five thousand. You drive a Benz S450 valued at ninety to hundred thousand."

McCooly took a black and white photo out of the folder and laid it on the table in front of Francisco.

"Who is this in the Bentley?" McCooly observed for any expression that might show on Francisco's face.

Closely examining the photo, Francisco hesitantly answered, "I need my glasses don't recognize them."

Leon slammed his fist on the table, "Quit fucking with us."

McCooly replied, "You know damn good and well who she is."

"You tell me then."

"Her name is Melon and she is your daughter from your mistress Susiana." Said sternly, McCooly.

"Without my glasses I can't tell."

Leon snickered, "Some father you are, don't recognize your own daughter..."

Francisco moved as if to get up out his chair in attack mode.

Leon got in Francisco's face. "Sit down, quit faking it."

"We were told Susiana was your wife but as we dug deeper, it came to our attention that she's been your mistress for many years. What do you have to say?" Leon asked with anger.

Francisco lifted his hands as if to say, "What?"

"I noticed the Bentley passing by your house. The driver acted like she was headed toward your place until she saw us on the porch and slowly drove by..." McCooly pulled out his note pad, pointed and read: *"Observation noted - A female driver in a Metallic blue Bentley Continental GT Lic plate # IFC2, unable to read other digits; passed the house on the 3200 block of homeowner Frank Ruiz. The driver curiously observed actions of officers McCooly and Sicardo."*

"If my daughter was driving an expensive car, what does that have to do with me?"

"Plenty," replied Leon.

"Officers, you're off track." Insisted Francisco.

"How does a guy making sixty nine thousand dollars a year afford to buy cars valued at about three hundred-fifty thousand dollars?" Leon asked.

McCooly pointed his finger at Francisco. "It's all about the drugs..."

"You're searching guys and there's nothing here."

"During our investigation I noticed a photo of you leaning against a blue Metallic Bentley. It bugged the hell out of me, because I recognized that car. I took the plate numbers ran it through our system and Bingo!" said McCooly.

Leon showed another photo, "And this is your daughter running a red light in your Bentley."

"See, same license plate, IFC2 on the red light photo and in this picture here, where you are leaning against the same damn car, same fucking license plates." said McCooly losing his patience.

"So? What does that have to do with anything?"

"How do you afford these cars and maintain a second family on your salary?" asked Leon, trying to maintain his calm.

"And why was your friend Terry Mitchell killed?" asked McCooly.

"You're the detectives, you tell me. And the cars and my personal life are not your concern."

"But they are. We believe, someone who knows a murder victim, such as you, who has expensive artwork, luxury cars, owning a double life and living above your means is a signal of illegal means or criminal activities," stated Leon.

"It's all speculation that can't be proven."

Leon leaning into Francisco's space, "Trust me, we will."

A knock on the door, Lieutenant Rory poked his head in the room, "Detectives a word please."

They exited the room closing the door, leaving Francisco behind.

"I just received disturbing news." Informed Rory.

"LT." Greeted McCooly.

"Your witness in the Dan White shooting just got shanked at county."

"Did he...?" before Leon could finish his question.

"He was DOA on arrival at the County General ER." Said Rory shaking his head.

"Damn." responded McCooly.

"What's with this Ruiz guy?" Asked Rory.

"He knows something of Terry Mitchell's case but we have no proof," replied Leon.

"Get the evidence. I want to see these bastards all locked up."

"Working on it LT." Said McCooly.

Leon and McCooly re-entered the interrogation room.

"If there isn't anything else, am I free to go?" arrogantly asked Francisco.

"We're done for now," responded Leon.

McCooly replied, "We'll see you later with an arrest warrant."

As Francisco walked out the door, he grunted defiantly, "You do that."

The door automatically shut behind him.

"I want that asshole behind bars," McCooly irritated said to Leon.

"We'll get him. We need to track down Monroe."

"He's out on bail and may have left town."

"If he's gotten the word that his partner in crime was killed in lock-up, he's probably running scared."

"He might be willing to be a little more cooperative knowing his ass is exposed."

"Let's start fresh tomorrow. I made a promise to have a date-night at a reasonable hour if I want to get some buttie."

In unison they slapped palms back and forth, singing, "Aint no buttie like off-duty buttie."

~

A hard knock on the door got an immediate response from Temoc, "What is it?"

A bald, tattooed street soldier stood in the doorway, "Juan Tequila is here."

"Ok give me five minutes then send him in."

Returning his attention to Maricela, Temoc said, "We have another shipment arriving in two weeks, be ready."

"No problem."

"Lay low for a while and wait for my call."

"You got it."

Maricela exited and few minutes later Juan Tequila entered.

"What's happening killer?" greeted Temoc, offering Tequila a chair.

"Everything is good *Jefe*, glad to be back in LA."

Temoc laughing, "What! You didn't like Big Sky Montana?"

"Not really."

"What about my boy Redneck."

"He's fucking crazy."

"Cross him and he'll kill your family down to your second-generation cousin."

"I'm glad no problems, everything worked good."

"Your crew's been working and earning your bones." Temoc looking at Tequila with stern eyes, "But you still have that problem with that *máyate*."

"What do you propose?"

"Rock his world baby making sure he never sees the light of day."

"OK, I'll get my homeboys together…"

"Temoc interrupted him, "Just get it done. I already took care of the one at county lockup for you."

"Who?"

"Omar."

"You mean Otis?"

Temoc snapped his fingers as he remembered the name, "Otis, that's the one."

"I'll take care of Monroe."

"Do I get a thank you for helping clean up your mess?"

"Thanks," answered a dejected Juan.

Temoc poured another drink downing it quickly then slammed the shot-glass on the table, "If I have to get involved you're both dead."

Tequila's eyes locked with Temoc's. "I got it."

~

On the balcony, sitting outside the master bedroom, smoking a petite cigar, Leon gazed at the stars and let out a gentle sigh.

"What's wrong *popi*? Is it still about that loyalty shit?"

He turned back to see Vanessa standing in the doorway; her silk robe opened exposing her nakedness.

"Damn, you are one fine...exhibitionist."

"We're hidden from the world."

"How long you've been standing there?"

"Long enough... something on your mind. What is it?"

"Nothing, go back to bed."

"One would think that after our intense conversation and our rumble, you'd be out sleeping like a baby."

"Seriously." He said, a bit dismissive.

"Is it work, me, what? Do I need to clear up more of the loyalty shit?"

"Nothing *mi Amor*."

"You talk in your sleep."

"Yeah."

"Who are you trying to protect?"

"No one, something from a long time ago."

"Wanna talk about it."

"No."

"Damn it Leon, talk to me! Something is hurting you, I feel it when you lay next to me, I can actually hear your pain when you sleep."

"Can't."

"You can tell me."

"No. Especially you." He said annoyed at her insistence.

"What? What does that mean?"

"I'm a cop."

"So!"

"You're a newsperson."

"And?"

"That's like a lion and zebra living in the same den."

She closed her robe as she was ready to step back into the bedroom, then asked, "What!? You can't trust me?"

"Can I trust you to keep quiet about anything I may reveal to you?"

She didn't answer.

They both stepped back into the bedroom. He sat at the edge of the disheveled bed, she remained standing

"As I recall, the last time I shared...it aired on the 10:00 o'clock news." Said Leon.

"What are you saying?" she said as she got a cigarette on top of the nightstand. She attempted to light the cigarette with that damn faulty lighter.

"Don't light that shit in here."

"It's my house."

He got up to embrace her from behind, she stepped to the side turning away from him.

"The unsolved Baby Girl Righteousness murder... presented by you."

"Oh, that one."

"Yes that one."

"I thought it was OK to talk about ...."

"I revealed more than I should have."

"So you're mad?" She turned to face him. The cigarette dangling from her lips, unlit.

"I'll take part of the blame."

He removed the unlit cigarette, tossed it to the floor and then kissed her deeply.

She then gave him a coy smile. "You know you can trust me."

"There are some sensitive things I cannot discuss with you. Do we have an understanding?"

"But with one condition?"

"No exceptions."

She gently kissed his lips then the soft inside part of his neck. She continued, "Hear me out Detective Sicardo. When you're ready and only when you're ready to reveal something to me, which I can share with the good people of LA, just make sure you come to me first."

He untied her robe. It fell to the ground. He kissed the side of her neck then lowered his head on her breasts and gently licked softly one of her dark nipples.

She put her hand between his *Jordan's*, "Oh my."
They both smiled.

He lifted her into his arms and took her to the waiting disheveled bed.

—

The following morning, Leon walked into the main floor of the precinct.

"How long you been here, Cooly?"

"Long enough for two sausage McMuffin with eggs."

"How can you eat that crap?"

"Easy, this is good shit."

"How did it go last night?"

Lieutenant Rory stepped out of his office, "Detectives. Sicardo, McCooly. I need a minute." He gestured to them from the doorway. Once inside, Lieutenant Rory got to the agenda at hand.

"Any updates on Monroe Jackson?"

"Nothing yet, LT.," replied Leon.

"And what about this Juan Pasquel?"

"Nothing either." Answered McCooly.

"What gives? We have had our share of some nasty shit come down on our turf. Don't tell me we have no results. No suspects and no arrests."

"LT., with all due respect we have several suspects."

Rory's voice roared, "What we have, is an unsolved murder of a family with a missing child in Culver City.

"We inherited that case," said McCooly."

"There's an Indian running around killing people and leaving his mark." Said Rory, pinpointing to the real reason.

"We have..." Leon attempted to add to the explanation.

"Let me finish. Then we have one of our own killed in cold blood by some gang banger named Vodka."

"Tequila... Juan 'Tequila' Pasquel," said McCooly.

Lieutenant Rory's voice elevated into another roar. "I don't give a damn what's his name. Find the bastard. He's a suspect in Officer White's murder."

"LT., we're on it," said Leon.

"Do we have anyone locked up?" Asked Rory.

"No," answered McCooly.

LT. was fuming while he asked, "Did an eyewitness to White's murder get shanked while under our watch?"

In a weak voice, Leon said, "Yeah."

Lieutenant Rory in a sarcastic voice, "Aren't the gangland killings out of control?"

"Yes." Replied McCooly.

"What the fuck detectives. We need some goddamn results and we need them yesterday!" The roar seemed to have been heard throughout the entire building.

"LT., we're working all angles," reassured McCooly.

"Get it done detectives." He waved his arm and with his index finger, he pointed both detectives to the door.

Walking out of the office, McCooly whispered to Leon, "I guess he didn't get any last night."

Once at their desks, Leon said, "Lets' hit the streets and follow-up with our informants."

"I'll work on securing a lead on Monroe Jackson's location," said Cooly.

"I'll get with Officer Yolanda Martinez, we'll check on the old man Cortez. He might have heads-up on how to find his nephew Pico Rivera."

Leon rubbed his chin as if thinking.

McCooly didn't say anything but noticed Leon's left hand twitch slightly.

OLIVER SIMS

25

Tequila was lying down on the couch trying to catch some sleep but the uncontrolled barking of Maricela's dog annoyed him into a hysterical rage.

"Shut that damn barking," yelled Tequila as he put a pillow over his own head to drown out the noise.

The howling kept on.

"Don't be screaming at my Ginger, she lives here, you don't," yelled back Maricela.

"My head is pounding." Tequila jumped from the couch, grabbed the 9mm on the table and pointed at the dog, "I'll kill you little motherfucker."

"Ginger, stop! Calm down girl," ordered Maricela grabbing the pet by the choker, "Aren't we grouchy this morning?"

"You'd be pissed too if you were gone for what seemed months on end... come back and had to sleep on a couch."

"What did you expect Juan?"

"That you'd be glad to see me." He said with anger in his voice.

"I'm glad you're safe."

"Things are going as planned. I thought you would be excited to see your man and we would make love like before."

"Juan you are not my man. We never made love."

"What was it then?"

"We fucked a couple of times, it won't happen ever again."

"What about all that shit I did for you."

"If you hadn't done it, Temoc would have cut out your heart."

With an overbearing sarcasm in his voice, he asked, "And how is Temoc?"

"Good... the homies are making deliveries, we're getting paid and paying our taxes to him."

"I don't like it."

"Take care of business or you're a dead man. And that means doing that Negro."

"Bitch," He yelled in anger. "I don't take orders from you." He caught himself at the last second just before he was going to strike her with a backhand whack.

"Go ahead hit me. I dare you."

"Don't fuck with me Maricela!"

She looked at him with dark cold eyes of a snake as if ready to strike. "I saved your life, asshole. Now call the fucking homies and get ready to go to work."

~

Leon and McCooly waited for Officer Yolanda Martinez to finish issuing her citation. Their unmarked car was parked at the northeast corner of Figueroa and Seventh Street downtown Los Angeles.

Leon stood in a corner in front of a street-vendor. "Do you want a dog?"

"No, I'm good." Answered McCooly.

"I love these bacon wrapped hot dogs."

"Do you think our boy in the Beamer is clean or will he have issues?"

Leon studied the young driver and said, "He's clean."

"What makes you say that?"

"He's Asian."

McCooly smiled and with a chuckle in his voice, "Sounds like your profiling bro'."

"No, just a summation."

"How so?"

"We're in the financial district, there is a young Asian driver wearing a white shirt, tie, a suit coat hanging on a hook in the back seat of a BMW 540i. He may have a poor driving record because of previous speeding tickets…"

McCooly interrupted, "You can add another to his profile. Martinez just handed him another citation," replied McCooly.

The driver took the ticket and carefully drove away as Officer Martinez walked over to meet Sicardo and McCooly.

"Appreciate you meeting us," said Leon.

"We're all on the same team." Answered Martinez.

"What do you have for us?" Inquired Leon.

"Word is Monroe Jackson heard about Otis Marshall and he's running scared."

"Where is he?" asked McCooly.

"My informant wouldn't give it up."

"We've got to find him," said Leon.

"My source tells me he is planning to skip bail and get out of town."

"We can't let that happen." Said Leon.

"It's a full court press to find him." Said McCooly.

Officer Martinez asked, "I'll check Mr. Cortez to see if he knows of his nephew's whereabouts."

"Press, the old man, hard. In fact we want to talk to him. Set it up." Requested Leon.

"Consider it done detectives."

～

Nervously pacing the living room, Juan Tequila walked to the kitchen, opened the refrigerator and shouted, "What happened to all the *cerveza*?"

"You drank it," said Maricela.

"Diego, go to the store and get some more," Juan demanded.

"What am I, your errand boy?"

Maricela went to answer her cell.

"Never mind, I need some fresh air." Tequila grabbed his gun tucked it behind his back and took his sweatshirt.

As he was about to step out, "Wait!" shouted Maricela after him, "It's the *Negron*."

"No fuckin way?"

"Asked for you." Maricela handed him the phone.

Tequila snatched it out of her hand, hesitated a moment wanting to sound unruffled, coolly he responded, "Monroe what's happening homie?"

Maricela listened closely but could only hear Tequila's responses.

"Yeah, I can do that. When? OK. Do you remember where we met for our first meeting? That's the place 7:00PM. See you *mañana mi amigo.*"

Maricela and Diego just stood there looking at Juan.

Tequila laughed. "He wants the Yeyo and the Mexican Brown deal that we were going to do before that cop came and fucked everything up."

Maricela smiled, sat on the couch, crossed her legs, lit a cigarette, sighed, "God is good."

~

The sun was settling in the west as Monroe Jackson drove east on Slauson Avenue. He turned right on Budlong Avenue and drove a quarter of a mile to the middle of the block. He slowly maneuvered his car onto the driveway of an abandoned building. Once he came to a complete stop, he sat for a few minutes behind the wheel rigorously scrutinizing his surroundings.

Observing the empty lot behind him and watching where several teenage boys were playing soccer on the field to his right, he deemed it safe to proceed. Still looking out his car window, he cautiously reached underneath the seat, retrieved his gun, then grabbed the backpack on the passenger seat.

As he stepped out of the car, he took a deep breath, then he heard a voice echo from the interior of the empty building, "*Señor* Monroe, what's happening?"

Monroe slowly walked inside and saw Juan Tequila standing in the shadow of the fading sunlight, leaning against his Honda CBK 1000 motorcycle.

"Hey man it's all good," answered Monroe.

"So you want to leave our beautiful city?"

"It's getting too hot up here."

"I feel you."

"You said you needed 50/50?"

"Equal split, coke and heroin."

"Got the money?" asked Juan Tequila.

"Would I be here if I didn't?"

Juan opened the gym bag on the floor and showed the two brick shaped packages. "In the clear plastic is coke, the Mexican Brown is in the tan wrapping." Flippant and sarcastically he added, "Don't want you to get confused."

"Man that was fucked up bringing the heat on us like that," said Monroe.

Juan didn't answer. He threw the gym bag at Monroe's feet. "Check it out homie."

Monroe knelt down on one knee, pulled out a knife and took a tiny morsel from each package tasting the sample on the tip of his tongue. He nodded in approval, "Cool."

He tossed the backpack stuffed with money to Juan.

"We good?" asked Juan?

"Yeah but you still haven't answered my question?"

"Monroe, now I understand what Temoc was talking about."

"Temoc? Who the fuck is Temoc?"

"He's *el jefe*. Sorry man it's only business." Juan took the gun from behind his back and shot him twice.

Monroe touched his upper torso. He was bleeding. "You motherfucker!"

Monroe fell lifeless to the floor.

Leon, Cooly and Officer Yolanda were staking that same empty building. They were around the corner on the east side of the street from where the shots were heard.

Within seconds, upon hearing the gun shots, Leon shouted, "Go! Go! Go!"

They burst out of the van with their guns drawn and ran at neck-breaking speed toward the building. It took only a few minutes to get to Monroe.

Leon looked up and saw the Honda CBK 1000 being driven across the open field. The motorcyclist leaned low to the side of the cycle riding fast at full throttle.

Leon fired his gun, missing the biker.

Inside the building, McCooly called for an ambulance.

Meanwhile, Leon called the dispatcher for backup with helicopter assistance, "Be on the lookout for a Honda CBK 1000, the driver is wearing blue jeans, red leather jacket and black helmet."

Three unmarked patrol cars following one behind the other flashed their lights and sirens, trailing the motorcyclist. As the patrol cars left the field and entered onto 64th Street, those same soccer players extended a tire-spike-chain in their way. Two of the cars spun out of control. The third vehicle smashed into one of them.

Precious time was lost.

The motorcyclist sped down 64th Street making a sharp right at the second corner. A large mover's truck as large as a two bedroom trailer-home, was parked smack in the middle of the street.

Another back-up police car, which had just arrived, was able to get the mover's truck to get out of the way. They followed right behind the motorcyclist, who meanwhile had just made a left turn on Hauser Street. The biker weaved and bobbed through several city blocks.

Two other police cars joined in the chase and with a helicopter hovering overhead, the motorcyclist pulled to the side of the road and suddenly stopped.

The police officers with weapons in hand ordered the biker to get off the cycle.

"Kneel on the ground and put both hands locked behind your head. Do it, now!" ordered the lead patrol-man.

The same officer handcuffed the biker, who was motionless on the ground. With the help of another policeman, they lifted the suspect off the sidewalk as if it the biker was a rag doll.

"Why are you assholes arresting me?" Shouted a defiant Latina biker.

～

The same large mover's truck, which had been stopped in the middle of the street, was now being driven down the 605 Freeway.

It got parked inside the warehouse where Temoc had been waiting patiently for it to arrive. His assistants immediately rolled up the back door of the truck.

Juan Tequila, smiling, was leaning cross-legged on his Honda CBK 1000 motorbike.

The assistants pulled the long narrow ramp from underneath the truck.

Tequila walked down the plank.

Temoc gave him a high-five.

"Nice going," said Temoc.

"If Pico hadn't stepped up and told us about Monroe getting with the cops, I don't know what would have happened."

"Your ass would be in my hands," said Temoc.

"His *tío* wanted him to leave the gang. But I knew he wouldn't ever. We're his *familia*. He would never rat me out."

"See what happens when you're organized and have loyalty to the *familia*. Nobody can stop us," said Temoc, proud.

"Now what!?" asked Juan Tequila.

"We stick to the plan."

~

Inside the precinct's interrogation room, McCooly stood with his arms crossed. On the opposite side of the table, in front of him, sat the Latina biker.

"Where did you learn to ride like that?" Questioned McCooly.

"My boyfriend."

"Who would that be?" Continued questioning, McCooly.

"You wouldn't know him."

"Try me."

No answer.

Leon stormed into the room holding a folder. Took a chair and sat across the metal table from her.

Leon enraged, said, "Maricela Barrone you're in a hell of a lot of trouble."

"For what?"

"I'm not in the mood for games." Said Leon.

"Seriously guys…" She wisecracked.

"I'm detective Sicardo and that's detective Mc-Cooly. You'll address us as such."

"Whatever." She answered sarcastically.

"Do you know why you're here?" Asked McCooly

"I should have stopped when I first heard the sirens." Brashly answered Maricela.

"But you didn't." Said Leon.

"I wanted to see if I could out run you guys." Audaciously she commented.

Leon's voice exploded, "Damn it! Quit with the bullshit." He pulled out a photo from the folder and placed it in front of her.

"Do you know this man?" Asked Leon.

"Nope."

"You hardly looked at the photo." Leon was starting to lose his temper.

"I saw it and I don't know him."

"Tell me about Juan Pasquel." Leon pursued with his questioning.

"Who?"

"Juan 'Tequila' Pasquel."

Laughing, she said, "I know Patrón and Don Julio Tequila but no Juan Tequila."

McCooly abruptly turned his chair around, then sat down again to face her almost nose to nose. Looking straight in her eyes, he questioned sternly, "You think this is some kind of joke?"

"I was reckless – sorry! Write me up, give me a ticket and send me to driver school, whatever."

Leon reached over and grabbed the arm of his chair, so his anger would flow through it.

"We don't take murder lightly." Added McCooly.

"I didn't shoot no one."

"Who told you the victim was shot?" Asked Leon.

Maricela didn't answer.

McCooly told her, "We know you were a diversion to let the killer get away."

"That makes you an accomplice to murder," replied Leon.

Pointing to the photo of Monroe Jackson, McCooly asked, "Why was he killed?"

"I don't know.

"Who is Temoc?" Asked Leon.

Maricela once again didn't respond.

Leon's eyes were fixated on hers staring directly into her line of sight, "Who is Temoc?" He repeated.

She needed to remain as cold as stone.

McCooly standing to the side nodded to Leon to exit.

"Sit tight Ms. Barrone, we'll be right back." Said Leon.

She threw her hands up. "Like I can go some-where."

In the hallway McCooly said, "She's lying."

"She was coached well. But the minute I mentioned Temoc, she lost her cool."

"She was frightened." added McCooly.

"Other than a marijuana possession charge in high school, she has a clean record. Keep her here for as long as possible. All we can do is write her up for the speeding ticket."

"She's dirty."

"I know but we don't have anything. When she's released let's put those bad asses, the Special Tracking Unit on her 24/7 and an all-out APP on Juan Tequila."

"I'm ahead of you, the APP has already been dispatched," said McCooly.

A patrolman approached, then said, "Lieutenant Rory wants you guys in his office."

~

Behind closed doors, Lieutenant Rory's was explosive. "What the hell happened? Forty thousand dollars from the city's coffer to capture a cop killer and what do we have?"

"LT., we..."

"McCooly shut up, I'm not finish. We don't have shit! Nothing! *Nada!*"

"LT., listen, we have..."

"Leon damn it! I 'm speaking. I don't want to hear anything you simpletons have to say, until I'm finished.

"Yes sir!"

The news services are having a field day and the brass is in my ass. What the..."

Leon interrupted, "LT. it's not over. Our informants got to Monroe who led us to Tequila. We'll get Juan Tequila and his boss Temoc."

"Who the hell is Temoc?" howled Lieutenant Rory.

"He's Juan's boss."

"You haven't answered my question. Who is he?"

"We're not sure yet," said Leon.

"How did this guy surface?"

"Juan Tequila mentioned his name, as his boss, just before he shot Monroe." Said Leon.

McCooly sat upright confidently in the chair and without a doubt, said, "As you recall, we had clearance to wire Monroe. We're on it, we'll track them down."

"What's the story on the woman biker?" Asked Rory.

"She's involved," said Leon.

"She's clean. She'll be released and we'll keep an eye on her around the clock," explained McCooly.

"It was an elaborate ruse, too sophisticated for amateurs. Definitely the work of the Cartel," said Leon.

"Before you boys left my office last time, you had said everything was under control, we would get Officer White's killer. Isn't that what you said, Detective Sicardo?"

McCooly replied, "We'll catch these bastards."

Sicardo stood silent.

"You're asses are on the line," belched out Lieutenant Rory.

26

"Bless me farther it's been a while," said Leon as he did the sign of the cross, inside the small unlit confessional.

Through the thin metal screen, the stately man opposite Leon, asked, "Is that the voice of Detective Sicardo or is my hearing playing tricks on me?"

"How are you father?"

"An old man like me is always glad to see a new day. And you?"

"I'm just checking in."

"Is this the day you rid your soul of those sinful deeds and receive God's grace?"

Leon smiled, "Like I told the priest back home as a kid in Colombia. 'Why confess to any other middleman when I can go straight to the source?'"

The priest jokingly said, "What are you trying to do, put me out of business?"

"Don't worry Father, the world is full of people who need your service."

"And what brings you into my parlor?"

"I'm just here for a friendly conversation."

"You realize they have professionals for that kind of thing."

"I'm an old school Latino and talking to a shrink is not my thing."

With a light laughter the priest said, "Too much machismo?"

Leon didn't answer.

"Still have those dreadful dreams?" Continued the priest.

"Let's just say they're a part of my DNA."

"What's on your mind?"

"What I am preparing to do."

"And what is that?"

"Kill someone."

"What did you say!?"

"In the line of duty some very bad people will be killed."

"You and I have talked on numerous occasions but you've never revealed pre-motivated actions to do your job. Why now?"

"A criminal enterprise consisting of narcissistic killers and sociopaths, drug dealers, are doing some atrocious things and it's going to get ugly before it gets better."

"What is it that you have always told me, to 'Protect and to Serve the citizens of Los Angeles,' it is your re-sponsibility and duty."

Leon remained silent.

"Do your job knowing that the Lord will protect you."

The church's atmosphere was impregnated with stale silence. In that quiet solitude, even a pin being dropped could be heard.

The priest broke the long stillness. "Is there anything else my son?"

"Wish me luck."

"I will pray for your protection. Go with God's speed."

"Thank you Father."

~

The walls of the room were painted light-blue and with motifs of white clouds, which seemed as if they were floating on the ceiling. Stuffed animals in different sizes, shapes and colors were neatly placed throughout the room.

Maricela cuddled her son comfortably in her arms, smothering him with kisses, as she walked back and forth within the confined space of her living room.

"I missed you little *papito*. *Mami* is sorry for leaving you but she had to work..."

Smiling with his pretty green-brown eyes, the baby looked up at her as if he had understood every word she had said.

"*Mami* did some wild crazy shit. And you know what? She loved it!"

The vibration of the cell on the table distracted her from that tender moment. She placed him in his crib and kissed him on the forehead.

"*Hola Papi*, I been waiting for your call."

"Maricela you are one bad ass bitch. A superstar! Brava," said Temoc.

"I will do anything for you - *papi*."

His voice expressed care and concern, "Sorry for the extra day in lock up. You got the money?"

"*Si,* Wow!"

"Just an extra token for a job well done."

"Through the lawyer, I got this cell phone, he instructed me to use only this one."

"That's right. When you talk to me or when we're discussing business only use this burner phone. It's very important you understand this." He instructed.

"Of course."

"They are going to be watching and listening to everything you say and do. Wait for my instructions."

"Did Juan make it?" Maricela asked.

There was a pause.

"At the questioning, you didn't give up any information, did you?"

"No, just told them what we rehearsed."

Another pause.

"What is it?" He urged.

"There was one thing."

"What? Speak up?"

She hesitated and was slow to answer.

His demeanor changed. "*Mujer*! Speak up."

"They know your name."

"What you do mean, they know my name!?"

"They showed me a picture of the negro Monroe and asked if I knew him."

"And?"

"I told them I don't know him... never seen him. They asked me two or three times and each time I said the same thing."

"Go on?"

"Then the detective asked me 'Who is Temoc?'"

"How many detectives were in the room?"

"Two, a *máyate* and a Latino.

"Was he Mexican?"

"No, his accent was different. Not sure what it was."

"Which one asked about me?"

"The Latino."

"Be more specific?"

"Just out of the blue he said 'Who is Temoc?' I told him I don't know anyone by that name."

"Good girl."

"But how did they get your name?" asked Maricela.

"Good question?"

"What now?"

"Keep a low profile. I'll contact you."

⁓

Walking into Eddie Cole's Tavern, Leon heard the melodic sounds of Jimmy Forrest's saxophone through the elaborate sound system. Forrest's clear, soft, serene notes of *Bolo Blues* sounded as if it were being played live.

Seeing Julio stationed behind the counter wiping down the surface of the bar, brought a smile to Leon. "I'm in the right place at the right time, how you doing *amigo*?"

Julio extended his hand to greet Leon. "Living the dream, my brother. What brings you back, business or pleasure?"

"Taking a brief reprieve to escape the madness."

"This joint is all about the luxury of living life…"

The music in the background changed from a delicate, bluesy saxophone sound to a swinging hard-core orchestrated Latin groove.

"Where else can you walk into an establishment and hear the spirited piano playing of Edie Palmieri belt out *A Night in Tunisia*, savor the taste of seasoned comfort food and enjoy stimulating conversations?" Said Julio. What's your pleasure? The usual *Four Roses*?" Julio looked with a questioning face. "Neat, if I remember right."

"Neat." Confirmed Leon.

"Coming right up."

"You got one of those Cubans stashed behind the bar?"

"I have a *Cohíba Esplendidos* or *Partagas D6*?"

"I'll take the *Partagas*."

"You have refined taste my friend. A very good bourbon and an excellent cigar. What's your taste-bud craving?"

"Papaya."

Julio gave a devious mischievous look, "Ah papaya, do you desire the *azúcar* of the fruit or the sweet nectar of a beautiful woman?"

Their laughter was contagious. A few clients at earshot started laughing as well.

"You are one crazy Cubano," said Leon.

"You started it," replied Julio.

Leon quickly reviewed the menu. "How's the *sopa rabo*?"

"It's braised and well-seasoned with Cuban spices in a red cabernet sauce. It's exquisite."

"And an extra order of sweet plantains on the side."

"You got it."

Julio poured him the drink and bend down to the humidor, which was hidden underneath the bar. He retrieved the cigar Leon had requested.

At the counter, he cut the tip, handed the cigar and lighter to Leon. "I'll bring everything to you."

Leon went to sit in the patio covered lounge. He positioned himself in front of the muted television, lit his *Partagas,* took a few draws from it and gulped some of the *Four Roses.*

'This is living.' He thought to himself.

He looked at his cell and scrolled for messages. He listened to McCooly's voice, *"Yo Sicardo, call me back, think I may have hit on something."*

Unable to connect with Cooly, he in turn, left him a message, *"Cooly I'm at Eddie Cole's. Hit me back."*

Next message was from Vanessa. *"Hi popi. You're so sweet. I can meet for about an hour during my dinner break. Besos."*

The hair on his arms stood up just by listening to her purring voice.

He breathed-in the aromatic vapors emanating from the refined liquor, took another sip and smiled with delight. He looked at the glass of bourbon with its golden-hue color and said out loud, "These are the little things of life."

He thought about James McCooly. *'We would always joke about being brothers from different mothers.*

Over the years, going back as far as being a beat cop on the streets, I've had quite a few crime fighting partners. Some were good, some bad, others I thought were straight out assholes. McCooly is different, really like a blood brother.'

He took a puff and followed the trail of the light blue smoke watching it evaporate into thin air.

He detected a familiar floral fragrance.

Vanessa was standing behind him. She said in that same sultry voice, "Can I interrupt?"

"How long have you been there?"

"Long enough to see you were deep in thought."

"You got here quick," he replied.

"You had said 6:00. Besides, I was excited to have an unexpected dinner date with you."

Julio walked in with soup and plantain, placed it on the table for Leon. "Here you go man." Then looking at Vanessa, "You are three times more beautiful in person than on TV."

"Julio you are always too kind. Thank you," replied Vanessa.

"What can I get you?"

Vanessa took a quick look at the soup selection. "Oxtail soup, with avocado and tomato salad, no onion please. Oh and an ice tea, no sugar."

"It'll take just a few minutes," said Julio as he went to place the order.

Vanessa kissed Leon on the lips. "You were in the zone, what were you thinking?"

"Cooly."

"You were thinking about him and not me?"

"*Mi amor*, I think about you, day and night."

"You were so engrossed?"

"If it hadn't been for him, I never would have made it as a cop. Hell I never would have made it through the academy."

"Really?"

"When I came to America, I was naive to the truth about American race relations. Institutional racism was a foreign concept to me."

"It's still alive and well. It seems, it still raises its ugly head and it is imperative that we fight it."

Leon was surprised at her comment. "You know what I am talking about?"

"I have already told you that my mother is redbone and my father is Mexican. I get it from all sides. As a kid, the whites, blacks and even Mexican didn't know what to make of me. I was just as confused as they were. I learned to maneuver in all three worlds. It's gotten better but it's still a fight."

Leon sipped his bourbon. "I was thinking how arrogant and superficial I was."

"Why do you say that?"

"I was twenty when I came here. It was the year after competing in the 1968 Olympic Games in Mexico."

She gently held his hand in hers. "You are always surprising me with tidbits of stuff. What was your sport?"

"I was on the swimming team."

She smiled, "That explains 'swimming with the sharks.' Did you win?"

"No. That's another story... for some other time."

"Sorry, you were talking about McCooly."

"In my country because I was in the Olympics, everyone treated me with dignity and respect. I was a hero. I couldn't for the life of me understand why Tommie Smith and John Carlos would protest and demonstrate against their country when it came the moment to accept their medals. At that time I looked down on them as arrogant, egotistical athletes. I carried a grudge against them for years as selfish, ungrateful blacks."

"What changed your view?"

"McCooly. He schooled me on being black in America.

"How?"

"It was living here and seeing America from within and not as an outsider or visitor. I got to witness and experience firsthand the unjust and racist treatment white Americans had toward blacks and other people of color. It wasn't until then that I understood the plight of Smith and Carlos."

"What woke you up?"

"It was in my cadet training, I learned the realities of what it meant to be relegated to the status of being nonwhite."

Julio and a waitress arrived bringing food and Vanessa's drink.

"Here you go oxtail soup, plantains and avocado tomato salad with no onions. Leon can I get you another drink?"

"No thanks, my brother."

"This looks wonderful." Commented Vanessa.

"Enjoy it," said Julio, as he and the waitress left.

As they were eating their delectable food, Leon continued, "My arrival in Los Angeles was extremely upsetting."

"How so?" asked Vanessa.

"I witnessed the mistreatment of Blacks and Mexicans in schools, the work force or even just riding on the city bus."

"Be grateful you didn't arrive in a southern state like Mississippi."

Leon continued, "In cadet school I received racial slurs and extra detailed work from the white superiors. They attempted to get me to quit. My English was extremely poor and they used that against me. I got blindsided by my Mexican peers."

"What do you mean?"

"They disliked me because I was Colombian and not Mexican. Their goal, like that of the whites, was to get me kicked out of the academy. I became isolated, withdrawn and wanted to quit."

"But here you are, years later!"

"I bonded with an unlikely source."

"Who was that?"

"The Blacks in the camp. Their determination was inspiring. They were going through hell, worse than me. They were only a few in my class but their resolve to take the bullshit handed to them was motivating. If it hadn't been for one particular cadet I never would have made it."

"Who was that?"

"It was James Arthur McCooly..." Leon took a sip of water, shook his head and chuckled, "He told me don't be their bitch. Suck it up man. It's only bullshit they are throwing at you. They aren't bullets or grenades from a hostile enemy. Don't give them the pleasure of you quitting."

"You guys been together all this time?"

"No. After graduation we worked at different precincts. We both became beat cops. We went through the entire LAPD system working robbery, narcotics, undercover and homicide, leading to detective."

"When did you become partners?"

"Three years ago. Both assigned to Hollenbeck Division."

"What was it like coming together years later?"

"Like twin brothers. We never missed a beat."

"You guys working on the latest shooting?"

"Which one would that be?"

"Come on, you know... Monroe Jackson. Got anything you want to share with me?"

"Yes."

Vanessa leaned toward into the table to hear what he had to say. Seeing that he wasn't volunteering any information, she moved even more forward in her chair, then, curiously asked, "What you got?"

"Your soup is getting cold."

27

Leon had just arrived and went to stand to the side of McCooly, who had discharged his 9mm against the paper-target practice victim. Given the size of the shooting range the amplified sound was acutely loud. They wore a headset to drown-out the noise.

Leon gave a thumbs-up signal of approval and yelled, "Good shooting."

McCooly shot the remaining four rounds and hollered back as he took off his headset. "Thanks, we're going to need it."

Leon did likewise then said, "I take it there is a reason for our meeting here this morning?"

"You know me, I like to be ready," replied Mc-Cooly.

"Be ready? What's up?"

McCooly pointed Leon to the entrance door of the range.

Detective Marcus Shaw had just entered and walked in their direction.

"I'll let him tell you," said McCooly.

"How you fellas doing this morning," nodded Shaw.

"Depends on what you got for us," replied Leon.

"He's been working magic on the computers. Share with him what you told me," said McCooly.

"I took the name Temoc recorded from the Monroe Jackson killing and entered it in our criminal data base. Nothing came up. Then I crossed referenced Temoc as a nickname."

"Anything come up?" Asked fervently, Leon.

"Slowdown partner, let the whiz-kid finish," said McCooly.

"I crossed referenced known nicknames in our criminal data base and got a ping. What popped when I put in the name Temoc? Cuauhtémoc."

"How do you say the name?" Asked McCooly.

"Kwo-Teh-Mawk."

"It sounds like a Native-American Indian name," replied Leon.

"That's affirmative detective. It means 'He who descends like an Eagle," said Marcus.

"Does our falling eagle have a last name?" asked Leon.

"His last name is Gutierrez. Cuauhtémoc a/k/a Temoc Gutierrez." Answered Shaw.

"What do we know about him?" asked Leon.

"His illicit activities started out as a kid and moved up the criminal food chain. He graduated and served time in San Quentin."

"Quentin is no joke." Said McCooly.

"Rumor has it, while inside Quentin he invoked two executions." Stated Shaw.

"Rumored? What happened?" Asked Leon.

"You know how it goes inside, nobody talked... authorities couldn't prove anything... so nothing happened." Marcus added.

"When was he released?" Leon asked.

"He got out in '98."

"By chance did you check any known individuals associated with Temoc while in Q?" Leon asked Marcus.

McCooly jumped in, "You ready for this?" He looked at Leon for a reaction.

"Temoc was closely associated with Hector Gonzalo Guerrera." Replied Marcus.

Leon wide eyed said, "Hector Guerrera, head of the Kaliffa Cartel?"

"What I've been saying all along, 'all roads lead to drugs, murder and Mexico,'" said McCooly.

"I did a little background research. Temoc status shot up giving him access to Hector after that first killing. And when the second hit took place; he was golden."

Leon shook his head.

They stepped back to the shooting lanes.

Leon refilled the magazine of his gun. He inserted it into the heel of his Glock, pulled back the slide, took aim and fired 10 rapid rounds into the middle of the paper-target. He pushed the lever and extended the target twenty feet further out then fired four more rounds hitting the midsection.

Leon extended the paper-target to its furthest point, took aim and shot the remaining two rounds. He retrieved it examining it closely. One bullet struck inside the silhouette of the head. The second bullet missed the target. He turned to McCooly and Shaw, then said, "I'll make good on that last shot. Let's go to work."

—

Within the precinct walls there was both disarray and orderly chaos.

Ladies of the night smacked and popped their gum as they explained to patrolmen that they weren't soliciting business but that they were just standing on the corner waiting for their Uber ride. Suspects in handcuffs were shouting their innocence. All this muddled unruliness was taking place just outside Lieutenant Rory's office.

Inside, behind closed doors was an unusual presence of calmness, no tempers flying, shouting or insults targeted by him toward his subordinates.

Rory was leaning forward in his chair fully engaged in the conversation. He made it a point to be alert to what was being presented to him.

"All three of you are in agreement that this Temoc character is an assassin for the Kaliffa Cartel?" he asked.

"No doubt," replied McCooly.

"We know by forensics evidence, he murdered the Terry Mitchel family and the drug dealer, Mario Lopez," replied Shaw.

McCooly added, "He also left his signature on the unsolved drug dealer's killing in Boyle Heights two years ago."

"And when he killed the Mitchell's and Mario he left the same markings." Added Leon.

Rory's voice was calm but with a tinge of anger, he asked, "Who the fuck is this guy?"

"Through science and technological advancements of computers this is what we know…" answered Marcus Shaw.

"I'm all ears," interrupted Rory.

"Temoc is an acutely accurate killer who has been leaving his mark on victims for several years…" Continued Shaw.

"The 9mm being his choice of weapon?" asked Rory.

"Correct but it's also the physical markings he leaves on his victims," replied Shaw.

"Is Temoc our Apache Indian?" Rory asked anxiously.

"Actually he's not an Apache, he's a descendant of the Chumash Indians tribe." Specified Shaw.

Leon and McCooly listened attentively, writing notes on their pad. It seemed like a ping-pong game, question and answer, between Rory and Shaw.

"How do we know that?" Rory inquired further.

"He lived on the Santa Ynez reservation near Santa Barbara."

"How long was he on the reservation?"

"He left at fourteen but it's important to note prior to leaving the reservation he went through a spiritual journey, a rite of passage…"

Rory sat up straight in his chair. "What does this have to do with anything?"

"Indians believe in animism, which encompasses the spiritual idea that the universe and all objects, animal, plants, trees, river even rocks have souls or spirits. They go through a process, a vision quest, a trance and connect with their power animal…" explained Leon.

Rory's demeanor changed, "Guys, where are we going with all of this?"

"This is a part of Temoc's profile. Animism, the spiritual world, coincides with power animals. A belief in supernatural capabilities that influences and empowers a person with dominating traits and characteristics of that animal." Confirmed Leon.

"Power animals or animal spirits connect and guide an individual, in this case Temoc, through different stages of his life. The eagle is his power animal. The wound left on his victims by the eagle's talon is his signature of the kill." Informed Marcus.

"Killing for the Cartel?" asked Rory.

"We don't know if he is an assassin for hire or a certified board member of the Cartel, but he's in it." Commented Leon.

"I'm getting the picture of the Mitchell family and Mario Lopez but what's the connection between the murders of Officer Dan White by Juan Tequila and him mentioning Temoc's name before he killed Monroe Jackson?" Asked Rory.

"We don't know. But it seems it's all centered on Temoc and the Cartel. We find Juan Tequila, we find Temoc," replied McCooly."

"And what's with this Mexican girl on the motorcycle?" Asked Rory.

"We know she's connected but we had to let her go, lack of evidence. When the lead domino falls, they'll all fall," said McCooly.

"Keep digging detectives. Get these sons-of-bitches off the streets. I want them brought down. Come to me with whatever you need."

~

Pico Rivera, Diego, Bulldog and about twenty friends were partying hard. While the roaring vociferous sounds of the bass vibrated off the glass windows, in order to hear one another they had to shout over the music.

Beer, tequila and other booze flowed like water. The place reeked with cigarette and marijuana smoke, and cocaine was plentiful.

A woman sitting on Diego's lap, put her arms around his neck and in a slurred voice said, "I love it."

Diego looked down her blouse and smiled. "Is it the party or me, you love?"

"It's both, *popi*." She answered as she kissed him.

Pico Rivera with a mirror balanced on his knees was snorting lines of cocaine. He grimaced each time and each time, the hit gave him an electrical jolt running through his body.

"Rivera, let me hit that," solicited Bulldog, who was sitting at the opposite end of the couch.

"I'm lit." Pico handed him the mirror.

Pico stood up but couldn't walk. His heart racing as he made his way to Diego. It felt as if he were moving in slow motion.

"Dude, I'm fuck up." Pico strolled and fell into Diego's arms.

"Homie you got to pace yourself. Our shit is pure."

Diego laughing, nodded toward a Latina who was standing in the corner, "She like's you bro'. Get that big butt *chica* to calm your nerves. She'll know how to put your ass to sleep."

He hollered like a wolf.

Pico stumbled toward the young Latina and grabbed her round-bubble-butt, "Come, I'll share my personal stash... with you," slurred Pico.

The two disappeared into a bedroom.

The song, *'Hot in here'* by Nelly, blasted through the speakers. Some started dancing to a sing-along. *'Feel like busting lose, it's getting hot in here so take off all your clothes.'*

One girl did just that, took off her blouse waving it in the air. Another removed her T-shirt then her bra, exposing her melon-size breasts.

The woman on Diego's lap kissed his ear then started to rub his inner thigh.

The party was hot and alive, like the fireworks on the fourth of July.

No one heard the hysterical screams coming from the bedroom where Pico and the Latina had gone to.

She yelled again, "Help me."

Frantically she ran into the living room. No one understood her cry for help.

It wasn't until she knocked the sound system to the floor that she got their attention.

"Fuck," yelled the DJ.

"What the...?" Moaned Diego.

The others groaned that the music had stopped.

She screamed at the top of her lungs, "Call 911."

Diego jumped on his feet, knocking the woman on his lap to the floor. "*Qué?*"

"Pico... Pico, I think he's OD'ing." Screamed Pico's Latina as she pushed Diego towards the bedroom.

Pico was flat on his back.

Diego could only see the white of Pico's eyes.

From the doorway the Latina was shaking as she looked at Pico's limp body. She started to scream hysterically once again.

Meanwhile, Diego slapped Pico's face hard in an attempt to get him to respond. He then shook striking him violently. Diego yelled. "Pico wake up."

Drooling from the side of his mouth, Pico moaned.

"Come on homie wake up," Diego shouted louder.

"Call 911." Yelled hysterically once again the Latina.

Diego shouted, "No. No cops or ambulance." He looked at Bulldog, "Help me get him up. We'll drop him off at Urgent Care."

They lifted Pico and took him to the car.

"Is he dead?" Asked the Latina.

"*Muchacha*, he looks dead to me," said one of her friends.

Once the Latina and Bulldog were in the back seat holding Pico, Diego sped away.

"Drive faster he doesn't look good." Desperately said the Latina.

They stopped in front of the Urgent Care Medical Center.

"Wait here," Diego said to the Latina.

Diego and Bulldog carried Pico's flaccid body out of the car. They laid Pico down outside of the entrance, on the concrete floor.

As soon as the automatic glass doors opened, Diego shouted inside, "He OD'd."

They ran back to the car and sped off.

~

Vanessa had received an unexpected phone call.

"I need to make up for my non-gentlemen behavior, not showing up at Cole's Tavern. Not my style."

"Mano!?" Vanessa was surprised to hear from him. After a few more pleasantries, she was even more surprised, "Come to your daughter's second birthday party?"

"Not as romantic as Eddie Cole's."

"Last time, you had said you weren't married."

"I'm not." With hesitation he continued. "She's adopted."

"Admirable... a single parent. And being a man..."

"In our culture we invite people we want to get to know or who we really like to our family gatherings. Brings us closer. You become part of the *familia*."

"I'm honored. Sure."

"I'll have my chauffer pick you up."

"Whaoh! A chauffer."

"The little perks when life is good to you."

"You never did tell me what you do."

"We'll have time for that. We're on then?"

"Yes, but I'd prefer to drive there. Text me the address."

Vanessa after having accepted the invite felt a bit uneasy and immediately thought of Leon. 'After all, besides the passionate lovemaking. Just like a lion, he doesn't let anyone get close to him.'

~

Inside the brick and mortar building in Ensenada, Mexico, mechanics were using state of the art equipment and tools to revive and refurbish back to life, cars and trucks. Sparks flew as the mechanic with his electric sander smoothed the edges of the fender on the vintage 1967 Chevy C-10 long-bed pickup truck. Riveting sound of lug nuts were heard as they were being removed or fastened onto tire rims of two cars suspended on a rack. With six work stations, the garage looked more like an automobile assembly plant than a repair shop. Large commercial fans stationed throughout the garage kept at bay the hot and humid 98 degree outside temperature.

Juan Tequila kept a careful watch from the hidden from view car-stall, where a red Ford Fusion was stationed. As soon as he was told that it was ready, Juan took the Saran-wrapped bricks from two nearby black garbage bags and quickly started to neatly position them inside a concealed compartment in the trunk.

The supervisor, a rotund man in his early thirties, walked over and checked Juan's work. "You're the bricklayer?"

"Yeah I'm the best at it."

"What about the sticky stuff?"

"Already placed the coffee grounds under the tin foil. *Hombre*, I know how to pack the shit."

"You're a *cholo* from across the border. First chance you get, you're back to Holly-woody."

"I love LA." Juan gave him a dirty look. "Why does everyone call you *Señor*?"

"How do you say in English - mister?"

"*Señor* – that's it? No first name or last name?"

"I'm a man of few words."

"When do I get out of here?"

"What… it's beneath you?"

"A *puta* could do this."

"You have another fuckin' car to pack and at this pace we'll never get our quota in on time."

"How many is that?"

"Need to cut and slice three cars a week... Sixty kilos exactly."

Tequila with a serious expression quickly did the numbers in his head, then bellowed, "Eighteen million a month!"

"Shut the fuck up."

"Man! Where do they all go?"

"Enough talk. Just be thankful for Temoc."

Tequila needed to know more.

Towards the late evening, *Señor* walked over as Tequila finished placing his final bricks in the last car of the day.

"He's always placing me in these small towns."

"I can't understand why you're in good graces in Temoc's eyes."

"I'm bored as fuck. I need some excitement."

"It's no small town, we have a half-million people."

Tequila laughed. "You've ever been to Los Angeles?"

"I'm stuck in here."

"Yeah tell me about it! LA's got more than three-million people."

"You talk too much."

"It's Friday, I'm going out to find me a *chica*, drink some tequila and let the sun bite me on the ass before sunrise."

As *Señor* was walking away, he turned to Tequila, "Yeah, you do that."

OLIVER SIMS

28

Hussong's Cantina, Ensenada, the oldest establishment in town, since 1893. An old wooden structure, sawdust-covered floors and where a nine piece mariachi band blared its music. Tequila was annoyed to no end. The night air, hot and sticky, with the exception of an occasional ocean breeze, gently swirled through the city. The coastal town known for its night life was packed with local patrons and tourists hopping from bar to bar.

'This shitty music sucks,' Tequila thought. He downed another drink, tossing a tip on the table and exited the cantina.

Walking on the cobblestone street, he staggered several times. His mind occupied on how to get what he was after - untamed sex.

The city by the bay had no limits on the amount of drinks one consumed, drugs taken or unfettered sex one may have chanced upon.

Sweat exuded through his pores. He noticed several women whose blouses clung to their moistened sweaty bodies. To Juan, it was sexy, a turn-on.

His roving look spotted two physically attractive women standing under a lamp post.

He sniffed some white flakes giving him a gnarled fantasy and a motivation to obtain whatever he desired.

'Tonight - I'm not going to pay for any *chica*.' He thought.

One of the two young women struggled trying to strike-lit a damp match.

He took a deep breath and after a few steps while trying to be a chivalrous gentleman, dropped his lighter. He stumbled forward, picked it up and with a quick flick, lit the damn thing.

"Here you go."

The one he helped light the cigarette, had sensual brown skin tone and in her tight fitting jeans revealed thick curves. Her burgundy red hair wet from perspiration clung to her nape. She wore Wicked-Dark Crime Valentine lipstick and flame-red nail polish.

Her friend had shoulder length blond hair with fire engine red lipstick and matching fingernails.

'My kind of *chicas*. Just like the women from West LA.' He thought.

"Where you girls from?"

"Guadalajara."

"I hear an accent," he said.

The bronze skinned *chica*, said, "We live in the US."

"We needed a little fun," remarked the one with the burgundy red hair.

"College spring break," added the blond.

"Can I buy you a drink?"

"We're good," said the burgundy redhead.

"Come on let's have a drink," insisted Tequila.

"We're going to the Blue Parrot."

"Never heard of it." Said Tequila.

"It's around the corner," said the blond.

"Great! Let's go," said Juan Tequila.

"No thanks, like I've said, we're OK."

"Two for the price of one?" Tequila couldn't resist the urge to ask.

"Looks like you had enough," said burgundy red.

"What's your name?" Tequila asked, looking at the blond.

"She's Borgoña, I'm Blanca." Mockingly said the bronze skinned woman.

They both laughed out loud.

Tequila followed them to the Blue Parrott.

~

The automatic glass doors remained open as Pico laid on the ground at the doorway entrance to the Urgent Care Medical Center.

"What are they doing?" said a male nurse as he rushed over to assist.

The same male nurse had seen two guys run to their car, jump in and speed off, but he couldn't get the plate number or make of car.

He shouted to the other assisting nurses, "Code Blue, Code Blue."

Two nurses on each side of Pico stood ready to lift him onto the gurney. Meanwhile a team consisting of a physician and two female nurses had arrived.

"Let's get him up," stated the doctor, "3, 2, 1."

The team lifted Pico onto the gurney. Within seconds they transported him to the ER trauma section.

"A male overdosed," shouted the male nurse.

"Do we know what drugs were taken," asked the African-American doctor.

"Don't know. Two guys dumped him here," stated the male nurse.

"Respiratory failure," reported the female nurse as they rushed Pico for examination.

"Need to intubate and get an IV started," commanded the doctor.

"BP dropping 40 over 30," said the female nurse.

"I see a fresh needle mark. Get me 5cc of Narcan, stat," demanded the physician.

"No use." Said the female nurse.

~

Juan Tequila with his two *chicas* walked in the Blue Parrott where a Mexican band was belting out guitar licks and pop rock tunes. This was the hottest spot on the square. The blue and teal lights with large silver balls dangled from the ceiling giving the place a '80s disco ambiance.

The place was overcrowded with tourists from the cruise lines, which had docked in the port for the night.

Tequila and the girls wedged their way to the nearest open spot at the bar.

The band was now playing Beatle tunes in English and Spanish. Everyone drank and danced, creating a contagious energy, which got everyone singing.

The three started bopping to the tune, "*I Want to Hold Your Hand.*"

Juan was sweating profusely after only a few minutes of dancing, he walked to the bar shouting to the bartender, "Modelo Especial and Patrón, for the three of us." With the *chicas* right behind him, they got served immediately. "Here's to fun in Ensenada," toasted Juan Tequila.

They clinked the shot glasses. They downed it and followed it up with the *cerveza*.

Tequila ordered another round.

As a table became available, Juan rushing to get it, knocked a drink out of the hands of a customer.

Without apologizing he grabbed a chair and sat at the empty table. As he placed the shot glass and beer bottle on it, he waved the girls over.

A tall American a few steps away, confronted him. "Dude, me and my friends been eyeing this spot for an hour."

"So!"

The two women arrived and placed their empty shot glasses on the table.

"I see you got reinforcement," said the tall American as he started eyeing Blanca, up and down.

"Keep your eyes in your sockets." Warned Tequila.

"Do you know this dude?" asked the tall American.

"Just met him."

"Stay and we'll buy you another drink at our table," said the American.

"You mean my table and my bitches," shouted Juan.

"What did you say?" said Blanca, shocked.

"Sit your asses down." Juan pointing his index-finger at the chairs.

Borgoña slapped Juan across his face.

Juan got up from his chair.

The tall American threw a punch knocking Tequila backwards.

Juan stood up and as he leaned on the table clutched an empty plastic beer pitcher and struck the American on the side of his face. Tequila then immediately grasped a beer bottle, broke it over the edge of the table and was ready to take the second swing at the American. One of the bouncers seized Tequila from behind. A second bouncer arrived throwing Juan to the ground. They rolled Tequila over onto his stomach forcing his hands behind his back and tied him.

As Juan struggled to get up, shouting profanity, Borgoña took a beer and poured it over his head.

"Now who's the bitch, asshole?"

She grabbed Blanca by the hand and stormed out the club.

—

Eyes still shut as he was coming out from a deep dream, Leon patted his hand under the bedsheets at an empty spot near him, feeling and searching for her.

The dark roast coffee brewing in the kitchen and the sizzling sound of bacon aroused his senses.

"Wake up Simba."

Upon hearing that soft purring sensual voice, he opened his eyes and quietly yawned extending his arms and stretching his back.

"A far cry from last night's roar." She leaned over and gave him a gentle kiss. "Very poetic." She continued, "I'd like to pick up where we left off."

"If you get under these sheets I'll be good for nothing, for the rest of the day."

"Crispy peppered bacon, Belgium waffles with strawberries, coffee and orange juice... waiting for you, sire."

After breakfast Leon hopped in the shower. The hot steam in no time created a sauna effect. He sang along to Carol Bach-Y-Rita, *Morning Coffee.*

"You're my morning coffee it's absolutely true I get all caffeinated just looking at you,"

"Simba, your phone is ringing." Vanessa brought him the cell.

The deep voice of a heavy Mexican accent, "Leon Sicardo?"

"Cesar?"

"I hope life is treating you well, my friend."

"*Amigo*, it's been a while."

"Too many. I have a package for you."

"I can't wait to unwrap it."

"It's not bourbon, it's Tequila Sunrise."

"What!?"

"We nabbed him."

"I can't fucking believe it."

"Yeah aggravated assault, saw your APP on him. I need your DA to provide us the proper paperwork, so I can release him into your custody."

"We can't do that," said Leon.

"What the fuck!"

"The process will take months."

"What's the urgency?"

"Kaliffa will get to him first."

"Then I need to get him out of general population immediately."

"It's Saturday how you're going to handle it?"

"I'll put him in quarantine."

"Thanks Cesar, call you Monday."

Leon was not aware that Vanessa was at ear shot from him.

"What was that all about?" asked Vanessa.

"Can't discuss it."

"Fine. It's about the cop killer?"

Leon didn't answer.

"With that look on your face, it's got to be something bigger."

"Can't say."

"Don't tell me, something to do about 'Baby Girl Righteousness?'"

"Where did that come from?"

"It doesn't matter. I'm doing my own investigation on this still unresolved case."

"Whatever!"

~

Temoc immediately greeted Vanessa. He introduced her to several guests, including Maricela and her little boy. Then proudly walked over to his adopted child.

Vanessa all smiles, took the child in her arms. She glimmered a smile.

Temoc gleamed a smile back. "You'll make a great mom."

Vanessa just smiled at the comment.

She gave a kiss on one of the child's puffy cheeks as she handed her to one of the nannies.

She looked around the living room for an instant, then at Temoc, then at the child.

Vanessa had recognized the Mitchell's girl.

She did her best not to show her nervous emotions going through her.

"Vanessa, you're alright?"

"I... yes, just let me freshen up a bit."

Temoc told the other nannie to show Vanessa where the bathroom was located.

Once inside, Vanessa locked herself in and immediately dialed Leon's number.

"Leon, I'm in trouble."

"What? Calm down."

Vanessa in a soft-low voice explained telegraphically where she was and how she had gotten there.

"Are you alright? Anything unusual? Any guards around?"

"I didn't notice." Answered Vanessa.

"Go back inside and after, no more than 10 minutes, make believe you have forgotten your cell in your car. Then take off immediately."

Vanessa followed Leon's instructions to a T.

After a few minutes, not seeing Vanessa coming back, Temoc went to the large semi-circular bay-windows.

Vanessa's car was gone.

He saw four police cars pull up to the front of his house.

Temoc thought, 'How could I've been so stupid to let my guard down. Over a woman.'

Temoc had no time to do anything but escape with his "adopted" daughter through the hidden back-passage.

~

Marcus Shaw and Lieutenant Rory were waiting for Sicardo and McCooly to arrive for the meeting at Rory's office.

Leon immediately said, "We got him!"

"Who's that?" Shaw asked.

"That little fuck-up Juan Tequila." interjected McCooly.

"How far is the DA with this?" Rory demanded to know.

Leon looked at McCooly.

"Well LT. it's like this…" said Leon.

"We were late because we were consulting with the DA…" added Cooly.

"When are we getting our hands on him?" Rory demanded again.

"It could take six, nine months to go through normal channels." Said Marcus Shaw, concerned.

"You know what the LAPD Protocol is for extradition from foreign lands." Added Rory.

"When Juan was arrested, he had marijuana and coke in his possession." Said McCooly.

"How do you propose to get him here," asked Shaw.

Leon opened a file. "Juan was born in Calexico, California. He's a US citizen."

"The Mexican government is not going to want to retain in their custody any undesirable US American citizen. We're going to do a handcuff exchange at the US Tijuana border," replied McCooly.

—

At Lavender Blue, Vanessa was waiting impatiently and different thoughts riled through her mind. She had purposely chosen this location, wanting to start everything anew with Leon.

"I'm glad you accepted my dinner invitation."

"Of course."

"Thought you might be mad at me for having accepted to go to that damn birthday."

"No. I'm just…"

"Sorry to interrupt. I haven't thanked you yet…"

"No need."

An awkward moment of silence.

"Oh Leon, wish things could have been different."

"Yeah, me as well."

She reached over with her hand opened.

Leon reached for his *Four Roses Bourbon*, which Vanessa had already ordered for him.

She withdrew her hand in disappointment. She couldn't look directly in his eyes. She held back tears.

"Leon, my Producer called me in her office this morning. I'll be hosting my own show on MSNBC… on the east coast."

"You're accepting?" said Leon, almost in an inaudible voice.

"Can't wait to start."

29

Yolanda Martinez arrived fifteen minutes earlier than everyone else at Police Chief Gary Maryland's meeting. Sitting outside the office already waiting were Leon Sicardo, James McCooly and Marcus Shaw.

Lieutenant Rory called them inside.

As Lieutenant Rory went to sit next to Chief Maryland at the conference table, he asked everyone to be seated.

I'm sure you're are all wondering why you're here," said Rory.

"I'll get right to the point." Said Chief Maryland.

The detectives perked up their ears.

"I am initiating a new unit at the LAPD," continued Police Chief Maryland.

They were all surprised.

"The new unit, will be called '*LAPD International Fugitive Apprehension Liaison Unit.*' It will be responsible for working with Mexico's Policía Fedérale in apprehending Mexican citizen who commit crimes in Los Angeles and return to Mexico for safe harboring," said Chief Maryland.

"That means working with the Fedérales when they're seeking assistance here. We'll also give our cooperation to them to apprehend those who have committed crimes in Mexico and flee to Los Angeles for safe keeping," added Lieutenant Rory.

"We want to curtail the criminal activities by the Cartel across the borders. So, we nominate Detective Leon Sicardo to head this Unit. It will be the responsibility of you three to cooperate with Detective Sicardo to bring this about." Said Chief Maryland as he looked at McCooly and Shaw.

"Sicardo, you and your team will be first responders when it comes to working with the Mexican authorities. We will have more detailed meetings with other department heads and with me to facilitate this transition. Officer Martinez you will be promoted to detective. Any questions?" explained and asked Lieutenant Rory.

"When do we start?" asked Leon.

"Effective immediately. And Lieutenant Rory will provide further instructions. Thanks for coming and good luck." Said Chief Maryland.

"You're dismissed." Instructed Lieutenant Rory.

Before anyone else, McCooly walked out of the meeting. The door slammed behind him.

Lieutenant Rory thought to himself, 'Your 'tude has always been your problem.'

McCooly was furious.

He couldn't believe that Leon had gotten the position as "lead" on the new formed unit. "Fuckin' country. It will never change." He said out loud.

"Cooly! What you're rambling about?"

"You never called me Cooly, before."

"A girl can change her mind. No?"

He observed her from top to bottom.

"Stop looking at me like that."

"Like what?"

"You know…"

"Today, you're flirting with the wrong guy."

"Am I!"

"Which way you're going?" Asked McCooly, with a seductive undercurrent.

He followed Dr. Liang's footsteps, as she made her way to the lab. And as she was about to enter, he held her back by her arm.

"Cooly not here."

"Where then?"

She led him in and locked the door behind her.

Without speaking a word they made their way towards a metal slab.

McCooly cast aside his shirt.

Dr. Liang pushed McCooly backwards onto her personal Medical Examiner's metal slab. As soon as his back laid on it, Cooly thought, 'Damn, this is just as cold as the reality of life.'

She straddled him, the heat between them built to an ultimate climax.

~

Later the same night that the Special Section was created, Sicardo and McCooly met at Eddie Cole's.

"I thought it was going to Marcus." Said Leon.

"What about... if it were to go to me?"

"I had no idea, you..."

"You know damn well I deserve it."

"I had no idea that Rory was going to appoint me." Leon said, almost apologetic.

"Even you, a legal immigrant is above me."

"Whaow, you're making this about race."

McCooly didn't answer.

Leon held back his thoughts on why McCooly had not gotten the position to run the Unit.

But Leon always felt that James' love for women kept him from obtaining his goals. McCooly had a knack for being able to interact and date two sometimes three ladies at a time. Even though McCooly was an extremely talented and responsible detective, this would distract him at times.

~

The large air-conditioned office in Tijuana, Mexico, was a sigh of relief for Juan Tequila; unlike the tight, hot and humid, cramped jail cell he had been detained in.

In spite of being handcuffed with hands to his back, Tequila didn't mind the discomfort, he could breathe easier in that cool air-conditioned room.

Officer Cesar Flores of the Policía Fedérale and detectives McCooly and Sicardo had made all the arrangements for Tequila's extradition back to the USA.

Tequila was guarded by two armed Policía Fedérale.

Leon immediately handcuffed Tequila and seconds later Cesar took off the wrist cuffs he had placed on Tequila earlier that morning.

Sitting in the back seat of an unmarked patrol car, Tequila was sweating but most of all, was fearful of not knowing his fate.

McCooly read the Miranda Rights to Tequila, then said, "Juan, you're in deep shit, my man. We suggest you cooperate with us."

Silence.

"Being a cop killer puts you at the bottom of the totem pole. Jail could be hell. You should reconsider your stance and talk," said Leon.

"What kind of deal do I get?" Asked Tequila.

"No deals being offered here. We can only suggest to the District Attorney that you've cooperated," Leon continued.

"Life in prison is better than the death penalty," McCooly stated.

"I'm fucked either way," said Juan.

"Cause and effect," McCooly replied.

"Who's Temoc?" Asked Leon.

"Mano Cuauhtémoc Gutierrez is an enforcer."

"Care to tell us more?"

"He's no joke. He'll claw you to death." Continued Tequila.

"What's with the talon?" Asked McCooly.

Juan took a few minutes before answering. "It's his symbol from the spirit world. He's an Indian."

"What else?" Asked Leon.

"Nothing else." Answered Tequila.

"Alright. Then tell us about the drug distribution." Continued Leon.

"They have drugs flowing from everywhere. They always have a clean-cut gringo family of four. There's always two kids with parents in the car crossing the border, all done with proper documentation."

"Isn't that risky?" Asked Leon.

"Not if you know what you're doing. There's even a distribution happening in Montana, right now."

"Shit, what else?"

"Cocaine is placed in new cars coming out of Mexico from the American Ford Motor plant. Some of the cars are driven across the border."

"Damn, coming from the Ford plant?" Asked Mc-Cooly.

"That's nothing. They package drugs in modified cars directly at the factory and once shipped and delivered to dealerships all over the US; the homies go and buy the car for $14,000.00 and have at least over $40,000 worth of drugs concealed inside.

"You did well." Said Leon.

"Does this help me?" Asked Tequila.

"Like we've said, we'll talk to the DA, see what can be done for you." Said McCooly.

~

Pupils dilated, heart thumping, lungs heaving, adrenaline surging, Leon's stomach and bowels were in turmoil.

Under stress and fearful that he'd have to pull the trigger, Leon thought, 'Now I have to kill this son-of-bitch.'

"Shit!" Leon said out loud.

A bullet ricocheted off the wall nearly hitting him.

'Never assume... assumptions get you killed,' he thought. Leon took a deep breath, took aim, squeezed the trigger and fired two more rounds.

Chamber empty.

Within seconds, Leon loaded a new magazine in his 9mm, locked it and got ready to chase after him.

As Leon peeked around the corner, he saw Francisco Ruiz on the ground bleeding from his wounds.

~

Francisco Ruiz handcuffed to a hospital bed was being interrogated by Detective Sicardo and Detective McCooly.

"How much cocaine did Terry Mitchell steal from Hector?" asked Leon.

"You guys don't know shit." Francisco Ruiz said with an ancillary smirk on his face.

"What's so funny?" asked McCooly.

"The Iraqi war."

"Huhh!" responded Leon.

"The most devastating loss for the Iraqi people, after the war, was the ransacking of their National Museums. The biggest trove of archeological and greatest loss of historic artifacts in the Middle East, was when the American Military regime found themselves that somehow these treasures went missing," explained Francisco.

"What's that got to do with Mitchell and the Cartel drugs?"

Laughing hearty, Francisco said, "You guys think you're so damn smart. Terry didn't steal drugs."

"What?"

"The US Arms forces were assigned to protect 28 galleries and 50 thousand irreplaceable *objet-d'art* and relics of the Iraqi's ancient civilization dating back 5,000 years. Instead they robbed the country blind."

Leon and Cooly looked at each other, then Cooly read from the file. "Yes, Terry was assigned to Iraq."

"Hello! Now you're getting the idea." Francisco stated with satisfaction.

"He stole artifacts?" said Leon.

"The Museum's entire card catalog system was destroyed making it impossible to identify what had been taken. Terry made millions selling these stolen precious heirlooms."

"Like the gold mask on your wall at home. From Iraq?" Asked McCooly

"We moved so much shit, do you think I remember such a trinket?"

"Why were the Mitchell's murdered?" Asked Leon.

"The *Lioness Attacking a Nubian*."

"The hell, what?" asked McCooly.

"It's a famous 8th century B.C. gold and ivory plaque. Priceless piece of statuary from the ancient city of Hatra."

"Still doesn't explain... Mitchell's and Kaliffa's..." Leon said, a bit aggravated.

"An imitation," Said Francisco laughing to himself. "It was a fucking imitation."

"Like buying a Gucci bag on a stand in Chinatown," replied Leon.

"Don't tell me, Hector got the shaft?" Asked Mc-Cooly

"Terry couldn't pay back the two million dollars." Said Francisco.

"He signed his own death warrant," stated Leon.

"Now you're thinking, detective."

~

Two years later, on the week of Christmas, on one of those very rare rainy nights in Los Angeles, Leon and McCooly met at their favorite watering hole. Julio greeted them with a hearty welcome.

Throughout the entire time, Leon as well as Cooly wanted to reveal what was on their mind.

"I've been tapped by the Police Commissioner of 'The Windy City.'" Announced McCooly.

"Congratulations!"

"I haven't accepted yet."

"Come on man, it's what you been waiting for. Isn't it?"

"I guess we created something bigger than us, these cities want to copy our Special Unit."

"We'll clean these streets, across the entire country."

"After all these years…"

"We had a good run."

"What was on your mind?"

"I'm going to Colombia to tie-up some matter that's been bothering me for quite a while."

~

The last time Leon had his feet in Colombia, South America, was when he immigrated to the United States. He had left it with anger and so much remorse at not being able to see Sophia at least one more time.

He had gone back to his barrio. Much had changed in Colombia but the people he had left behind still remembered Darcia's "young man."

Leon still mistrusted the authorities in his country and didn't want them to know that he was looking for the Linstrem's.

Finally, Leon one day, found an older man in the barrio where Leon had lived who had been one of the few persons Ludwig had befriended.

"My good friend Linstrem... God rest his soul. FARC soldiers."

Leon had understood what he was alluding to.

"And Sophia?" Leon asked anxiously.

"Sad, very sad."

"Also...?" Leon couldn't get the words out.

"Would have been better for her..."

"Don't tell me..." said Leon anticipating the worst.

"In front of Ludwig's eyes as he was being tortured to death, she was raped by three soldiers. Poor thing."

"Where's she now?"

"Bogotá Mental Asylum."

~

Until he had met the older man in the barrio, it had taken Leon almost a year to find Sophia Linstrem.

An uneasiness had lingered as if tormenting his soul the entire day. Leon walked in the Asylum on a hot and muggy afternoon.

He wanted to see Sophia as quickly as he could.

The attending nurse pointed to a decimated hunched-over woman sitting on a wrought-iron bench in the well-manicured gardens.

"Sophia, someone's here to see you." Announced the nurse.

No answer.

The nurse whispered to Leon, "I told you she's been like this for all these years."

A wrenching grip on his heart was making him choke on his own words. "Can I sit here with her...?"

"It's been no use..."

"Please, alone."

The nurse annoyed at Leon for not heeding to her words.

Leon followed the nurse with his eyes as she walked away.

"Hi, Sophia."

Sophia did not move.

"Sophia, it's me... Leon."

She had shifted, not even a millimeter.

Leon cupped his hand under her chin, gently lifted her head so he could look into her eyes.

They gazed out at a fixed point in front of her.

Leon gently caressed her cheek.

He sat next to her for quite some time, just holding her hands in his.

"I'm sorry, Sophy... I'm really so sorry."

The sun was setting, Leon softly kissed her forehead.

He quietly walked away.

A few moments later, Sophia seemed to have heard Leon's voice in a gentle breeze, which hushed a lock of hair over her eyes. An almost muted word... was whispered in that same breeze...

"Leon..."